THE SENSITIVE

SYDNEY JAMES CARD

THE SENSITIVE

PART ONE:

BE VIGILANT

CHAPTER 1:

BEWARE THE HUNTER

MAY 2111

Janet Hodgson was always vigilant as she roamed about the dark wood – as part of their cat and mouse games. Janet was fourteen and her brother was sixteen. She was just under six foot, she had a slim figure and long athletic legs. She had short sandy hair and brown eyes, she wore a green blouse and a brown skirt – she hoped her clothes would blend in with the hues of the wood. Her keen senses were alert for any sound that her brother might make – in his effort to catch her unawares.

Jeremy Hodgson kept pace with his younger sister. Keeping his eye on her as Janet moved through the wood. Suddenly she stopped, and Jeremy waited for her to move off again. He would wait for the right moment to pounce on his unwary victim. The games sometimes lasted a long time, but they never tired of them. They both enjoyed the games tremendously as they tried to outfox each other.

Janet stared at the gaps between the trees ahead of her. She had seen something flash at speed across her path. It was too blurred to see what it was. She decided to move off through the wood, taking a different direction to the one she had been following. She kept in the shadows as she knew her brother would not be far away. She moved slowly amongst the trees. Unknowing she was being watched by someone other than her brother. The boy was intrigued by their antics, the strange games they played in the woods. He had seen the thing the girl had seen, rushing through the woods. It had never bothered him, so he ignored it. The girl was very watchful – though even that would not get you out of trouble, but he had to admit the girl was good.Jeremy got up and moved off and followed behind his sister. He suddenly saw movement to his left and he ducked down and gazed in that direction. He was just in time to see a boy move behind a tree.

Someone was watching them. Jeremy kept low and moved away and searched for his sister.

Janet stopped again as she spied the blurred image dart across her path. A lot of strange things happen in the wood and this was the strangest. She hadn't seen anything like it – she could not believe a being could move so fast unaided. Janet wished it would stop moving so she could get a better look at it. It was all she could see now – a grey blur. Janet kept moving eastward through the wood; she stopped on occasions to see if she could detect her brother nearby. Janet went past her cottage – which was just inside the tree line – and emerged from the wood. She gazed up at the cliff that rose in front of her. At the top of it was a tall electrified fence that surrounded a collection of long single-storey buildings.

Janet turned and faced the wood and she saw Jeremy emerge from the tree line. She went to her brother and told him – about what she had seen in the wood. Jeremy stared at his sister sceptically.

"You don't believe me – but it is true – you know I would not lie to you," Janet pleaded.

Jeremy smiled at his sister – he assured her – he would believe her whatever she said.

"We know strange things happen in the dark wood – obviously there is something going on in there," Jeremy said.

Janet nodded her head and turned and started climbing the steep cliff. Jeremy followed behind her – as he wondered what she had in mind. Janet reached the top and stood at one corner of the boundary fence and Janet wondered what sort of people worked there and what kind of strange experiments were done there. Jeremy stood behind her as she gazed at the people in white coats milling around the compound beyond the fence.

"You shouldn't loiter here too long – someone may come out and drag you in and do strange experiments on you," he said.

Janet turned and smiled at her brother, then ran off down the slope and made for the wood. Jeremy did not run after her – as he knew he had no hope of catching her – as her legs were longer and she could run faster than him. Janet entered the wood and made her way home. Jeremy found her in the kitchen, making herself a sandwich; Jeremy made some coffee.

"Do you really think they do strange things at that place?" Janet asked.

"I don't know – Melissa won't tell me what goes on in there," said Jeremy.

The back door opened, and a girl walked into the kitchen; she wore a green and white striped dress.

"Hello Ros," Janet said.

Rosalind Taylor lived in a cottage close by and often came to see them – she was a year younger than Janet.

Jeremy told Rosalind about the strange thing Janet had seen in the wood. Rosalind had seen nothing like the description of what Janet had seen.

"Do you think it's a living creature?" Janet smiled at Rosalind and nodded. "Though I don't know of anything that can move that fast."

Jeremy told Rosalind about the boy who had been watching them in the woods. She had seen him and told them the boy lived in a cottage on the other side of the wood.

Abigail Waldron walked out of the back door, carrying a large bath towel, which she laid out on the middle of the large expanse of lawn. She wore a lime green bikini; she lay on her back and gazed up at the clear blue sky; it was a warm sunny day. At the rear of the lawn was the line of trees that showed the start of the large dark wood. The boy emerged from the trees and spied the girl lying in the middle of the lawn. He walked down the lawn and approached the girl.

Abigail looked up and smiled. "I was wondering when you were going to approach me," she said.

She sat up and smiled at him. "I don't bite."

"You are very beautiful," the boy said.

He was tall, lean and handsome, the kind of boy, she liked.

Abigail stood up. "Thank you. Mother won't be back for a while, so we have plenty of time to have some fun."

Abigail walked back to the house and the boy followed her; they went in through the back door and she took the boy up to her room.

CHAPTER 2:

A GRUESOME DISCOVERY

Melissa Davis kept kicking at the dark earth as she made her way through the wood. She listened to the sounds of nature moving around her. Suddenly the tip of her left trainer hit something hard; she knelt and dug in the earth and her seeking fingers found something round. Melissa dragged it out of the earth and stared in horror – it was a skull; two vacant eye sockets stared at her accusingly.

Why did you do it?

Melissa dropped the skull and stood up. "It wasn't me."

Melissa turned and made her way out of the wood – when she moved out of the tree line someone grabbed her. She stared at the smiling face of Adam Williams.

"Are you all right, Mel?" he asked.

Melissa told him what she had found in the wood.

"I saw a dark figure moving through the wood – but I did not identify who it was," Adam said.

They walked back to the installation and Melissa went to her accommodation dwelling. She went to her mother's study.

Marina Davis was sitting at her desk and when her daughter appeared at the door she saw by the expression on Melissa's face that something was wrong.

"Are you coming here to tell me what is wrong – or are you going to shout across the room?"

Melissa moved slowly towards her mother. When she was near enough, Marina grabbed her right wrist.

"He's dead, Mother."

"Who is?" Marina asked, mystified. "Brian Scott, I found his shallow grave in the woods – he was murdered."

Marina stood up; she was shocked. She knew Melissa would not tell tales. They left the accommodation dwelling and made for the main building in the centre of the compound – it was a long single-storey structure. They entered through the entrance doors and moved down a short corridor in front of them, then they went through a doorway on the left; which took them to the offices.

Dr Elizabeth Wilkinson was the head scientist in the Installation – she had been friends with Marina since university. Elizabeth had got her the post at the installation – Melissa came with her so Marina could keep an eye on her. Melissa was studying the sciences and she enjoyed the work Dr Wilkinson gave her. Melissa told her what had happened to her in the wood.

DS Martin Sanderson drove the car up to Cook's Farm and parked it alongside the other police vehicles. DI Peter Hunter got out of the car and PC Rachel Robertson approached him as DS Sanderson came alongside him. She guided them to the crime scene – they walked to the wood and entered the tree line. When they reached the shallow grave, the skeleton was uncovered of earth and the forensic pathologist was knelt beside it. A girl and a woman were standing close by. The girl approached DI Hunter – the bright brown eyes stared at him, evaluating him; to see if his intelligence was equal to her own.

The dark stranger had a streamlined handsome face and the greys were as inquiring as her own as he returned her stare.

"I am Inspector Hunter – this is my sergeant, Martin Sanderson."

Melissa smiled. "You have the right name – you are a hunter."

She told him how she had found the body - she told him about Brian Scott, and she had no idea who would have wanted to harm him.

"How do you know the body is his?" DI Hunter asked.

"I just know it is Brian's remains – he has been missing for three years," Melissa said.

"I would say it was the killer's first kill," Melissa added.

"What else?"

The intelligent young girl intrigued him.

"This person wanted to find out if they could kill someone and Brian unfortunately got in the way," she said.

"I don't suppose you could provide us with a name of the killer?" DS Sanderson said.

Melissa turned to him and smiled. "Not yet – it could be a male or female."

Melissa flexed her left arm and put her right hand on the bicep. "I'm strong enough to subdue Brian. I am a big girl and it's not fat."

DI Hunter looked the girl over – she had a fuller figure and he could see she was fit and active and had no fat on her.

"If someone calls you fat – I'd arrest them," DI Hunter said.

Melissa gave him a smile – she liked the police inspector.

"Only I know I had nothing to do with Brian's death."

Marina placed her hands on her daughter's shoulders. "I know you couldn't harm anyone."

John Walsh stood up and faced DI Hunter. "The neck was broken – very professional." "Dr Wilkinson is waiting for you – she will cooperate with your investigations."

DI Hunter nodded and thanked her; they made their way out of the wood and went up the cliff towards the Installation.

A group of teenagers sat at their desks – four boys and four girls. Dr Wilkinson stood by the door as she waited for the police to arrive to question the assembled group. They gazed at each other to see who looked guilty.

The door opened, and Melissa entered the teaching room, followed by the two police officers. She went to her desk. Celeste Barnet sat on her right – she was tall and slim with short blonde hair and sparkling blue eyes; she was Melissa's best friend. On her left sat Nigel Barnet.

"Have you been told?" Melissa asked.

Celeste nodded. "I know it wasn't you and I shall tell the police that."

"I told them I couldn't think of anyone who wanted to harm him."

Brendan Goodman sat behind them. "It might not be one of us who killed Brian."

Melissa turned and stared at him – she was not sure of him. Brendan was secretive and did not give them much information about his past. He worked with her mother on her research – she did not know what it was as Marina told her daughter it was top secret.

"We would be the first suspects – then the scientists," Melissa said.

Brendan gazed at her pretty face and focused on the bright green eyes. A smile appeared on his lips.

"I suppose I am your first suspect, Mel?"

Melissa grinned at him – he knew they were suspicious of him.

"You said it," Melissa said.

Tabitha Dawson was fourteen – she worked with Brendan – she was of medium height with long black hair. She had a mischievous character. She sat in front of Melissa, then she turned to them.

"One of us might be next for the chop," she said.

"That's a sobering thought," Celeste said.

Tabitha giggled. "I thought you'd like it."

Dr Wilkinson called Nigel to the front desk. He sat down and faced DI Hunter – as Nigel was sure he was the senior officer.

DI Hunter studied the teenager's face as he asked Nigel about his feelings towards the murdered girl. When he had all he could get from Nigel, DI Hunter let Nigel go back to his desk. His sister Celeste got up and walked to the front desk and sat down and faced the two police officers. She told them what she knew of Brian – she did not work with him – as she worked in the genetics laboratory with her brother and Melissa. DI Hunter let her go. He saw the others one after the other. Brendan Goodman sat back and surveyed the proceedings closely. He could hear what was being said. When it was down to the last two, Melissa turned to Brendan and he shook his head; she smiled and got up and walked to the front desk. DI Hunter gave Melissa a friendly smile as she sat down.

He questioned her about Brian Scott and got similar answers to the others. The girl was honest in her replies to his questions and was eager to help him. Melissa did not know of anyone who wanted to harm him; so, she supposed Brian had seen something he should not have done.

Melissa turned her head and gazed at Brendan Goodman who was sat at the back of the room, then she turned back to DI Hunter.

"You'll have trouble with that one – we can't get a lot out of him – he knows how to get information out of you, without giving much about his life," Melissa said.

DI Hunter smiled. "I've met a few like him."

Melissa stood up and moved to the side of the room and gazed out of the window. Brendan got up and walked to the desk and sat down. He stared at DI Hunter's face as they sat facing each other. Brendan had a good guess at what Melissa and the police officer were talking about – he was good at that, watching people and working out what secrets they had.

"I wasn't here when Brian disappeared – I was told about it when I arrived," Brendan said.

"Had you met him?"

Brendan nodded. "We all met before we came here. We all were selected from various schools around the country. If you want to know what we are doing here – you'll have to ask Dr Wilkinson."

"Melissa tells me you are very secretive about your life."

Brendan smiled. "Mel is very bright and inquisitive about the world around her – she is very perceptive. I watch people – I don't kill them."

DI Hunter believed him – the boy was more interested in talking about other people than talking about himself.

"Have you any ideas who may have killed Brian?"

"I don't know who he had trouble with here – he could have been killed by someone outside this compound," Brendan said.

"We will consider that – but we have to start here and question the people who knew him," DI Hunter said.

"If I suspect anyone, I shall let you know," Brendan told him.

"Thank you – that will be all."

Brendan stood up and left the room. DI Hunter turned to Dr Elizabeth Wilkinson.

"Can I talk to the scientists who work here?"

She nodded and called Melissa over and told her to fetch Dr Gilligan, then Dr Wilkinson sat at the table. "We'll cooperate fully with your investigation," she said.

CHAPTER 3:

BAD DREAM

Melissa Davis made her way through the trees; the sun flickered through the branches – her keen senses told Melissa there was a mystery to be solved. She was sure there were more bodies buried in the wood, that Brian Scott was not the only one. She gazed down at the ground under her feet as she slowly moved forward. Melissa stopped as a strange whispering sound came amongst the trees – on her left. She changed direction and saw a tall dark figure move quickly out of her path. Melissa made a rush after it and she tripped and fell flat on her face. Something landed on her back and she was struck on the back of her head – knocking her out.

Melissa woke and got out of bed – the dream haunted her mind. She went to the bathroom and had a shower, then she got dressed. She went to the study and she put a hand to her mouth to stifle a scream. Her mother lay on the floor – Melissa rushed to her and knelt – she saw the neck was broken. The killer had struck close to home and she had been unable to protect her mother.

"I'm going to get revenge for this – whatever it takes," Melissa vowed.

Melissa rushed out of the quarters and went to security to tell them of the murder.

CHAPTER 4:

LURKER IN THE DARK

Detective Inspector Peter Hunter expected the worst when he was called back to the Installation. He hoped the victim was not Melissa or any of her young friends. Detective Sergeant Martin Sanderson parked the car by the main single storey building in the centre of the compound. DI Hunter felt relieved when he saw Melissa walk towards the car. A tall, older girl in a white lab coat was with her. Dr Claudia Hodge introduced herself and told him about the murder of Melissa's mother. He was shocked to hear that, and he gave his condolences to Melissa.

"Mother had no enemies – there was no reason to kill her – like Brian, unless the killer struck because I found where he was buried," Melissa said.

DI Hunter left them and walked towards the quarters. DS Sanderson stayed behind to question Melissa – when she was ready. At the crime scene, the forensic team were at work: Dr Walsh the pathologist was studying the body; the photographer was taking pictures around the room. Marina Davis had suffered a blow on the back of the head – caving in the back of the skull – and her neck was broken.

"I wonder why she was killed twice."

Dr John Walsh stared up at him. "Perhaps the killer had to hit her on the back of the head – before he could use the favoured way of killing; then decided to break her neck anyway."

They sat in Dr Elizabeth Wilkinson's office. DS Sanderson had his notebook out and waited patiently for Melissa to tell him what she knew of her mother's murder. Dr Claudia Hodge sat next to the girl – they gazed at each other – then Melissa turned to DS Sanderson and told him about her dream and how she found her mother's body.

"The killer might have been coming for me – because I found where Brian was buried, and Mother got in the way," Melissa said.

"He could have killed the both of you," DS Sanderson said.

"The killer was male – I had seen him moving about the wood."

"Who was it?"

"I saw a tall, dark figure – I did not see his face – Adam saw him too, but did not recognise him," Melissa said.

DI Hunter entered the room and Melissa turned to him. "There are people here who are very secretive about their past lives. I ask myself – what are they hiding?"

DI Hunter smiled at that – being in a secret installation – there were things here he would not be able to inquire about. DI Hunter turned to Dr Elizabeth Wilkinson and asked her if Brendan Goodman was about – because he wanted to speak to him first.

"Do you see him as a suspect?" Melissa asked.

Hunter shook his head. "He doesn't seem to me to be a killer – I've been told Brendan has been working for your mother for some time – so if he was going to kill her, he would have done it by now."

Melissa gave him a smile and told him she would go and get Brendan. She left the main building and moved towards the two buildings opposite – the left was where her mother had done her research. Brendan would be there, along with Tabitha and her friend Susan Bishop. Melissa entered the building and went to the laboratory. Tabitha looked up and stared at her.

"Is Brendan around?" Melissa asked.

"He's in the office. What's he done?" Tabitha inquired.

"Nothing yet," Melissa said and walked across the room and entered the office.

Brendan looked up as she approached the desk.

"What can I do for you, Mel?"

"The nice police officer wants to speak with you," Melissa informed him.

Brendan Goodman stood up and went around the desk. He was ready to face the police a second time; he was impressed with the way DI Hunter worked.

They walked out of the building. Brendan told Melissa how sorry he was about the death of her mother. She did not say anything – she hoped he had nothing to do with it – Melissa did not like the idea of working with a homicidal maniac.

Brendan walked into the interview room and sat at the desk and faced DI Hunter; Melissa stood behind him. He assured the police inspector that he had nothing to do with Marina Davis's death, that he worked well with her and not a bad word had passed between them.

"Where were you on the night she was killed?"

"Marina Davis left the laboratory in the afternoon – then Susan and Tabitha and I finalised the day's work. We talked some time after that – then we went back to our quarters," Brendan explained.

Susan Bishop came in next and collaborated Brendan's story. When Brendan left the room he found Keith Watson outside.

"You haven't been arrested then?" he inquired.

Brendan shook his head. "I haven't killed anyone."

He was not sure Keith could say the same.

Tabitha Dawson was working in the laboratory – now she was working alone, she wished her friend Susan was with her or Brendan; she knew they were helping the police with their enquiries – she was sure Brendan had nothing to do with Melissa's mother's murder. Suddenly the lights went out – making her jump.

"Who's there?" she called out.

She made her way slowly towards where she knew the door was, making sure she did not knock anything over. Tabitha was sure there was someone else in the laboratory with her – but she could not hear them. Suddenly someone grabbed her arm.

"Don't be alarmed – I'm not going to harm you."

The gruff voice was male but she could not recognise it.

"What do you want?" Tabitha asked.

It was too dark for Tabitha to see who had hold of her.

"I just want to know what you are going to tell the police."

The man kept a tight hold on her.

"I can't say a lot – I have no idea who killed Marina."

Tabitha had a horrible idea. "I hope it wasn't you who killed her."

"It would be bad for you if I had."

Tabitha could not argue with that. "Do you know who did?"

"Not yet – perhaps it was the same person who killed Brian Scott."

The man let go of her wrist and a moment later she heard the door slide open and then close.

Tabitha turned on the lights and a moment later the door slid open and Brendan walked in. Tabitha told him what had just happened to her and asked if she had seen anyone on his way in.

Brendan shook his head and told her to tell the police about it. She left the building and went to the main central building and made her way to the interview room. She entered the room and saw Melissa standing by the desk. She went to her and gave her a hug.

"I'm very sorry about your mother, Mel."

Tabitha sat at the desk and faced DI Hunter and told him what had just happened to her in the laboratory.

"Did you recognise the voice?"

Tabitha shook her head. "He just wanted to know what I was going to tell you."

"Brendan has just left here – could it have been him?" Melissa asked.

Tabitha turned and faced her. "It was not Brendan."

"I hope you are right, Tabs," Melissa said.

Tabitha turned to DI Hunter. "Marina was called away late in the afternoon – by phone – her voice sounded urgent. I could not hear what was said. Brendan took charge and Susan and I got on with our work."

"Have you any idea who she was speaking with?" he asked.

Tabitha shook her head. She left the building and found her friend Susan outside waiting for her.

"How did it go?""All right. I wonder who is going to be next," Tabitha said.

Susan hugged Tabitha. "I'll protect you, Tabs."

After the interviews were over, Melissa sat in the chair and faced DI Hunter.

"What do you think?" he asked.

"I haven't any ideas yet – we'll have wait until the forensics come in," Melissa said.

"I hope we get more information from this crime scene than what we got in the shallow grave."

"The killer is careful – we should expect that," Melissa said.

"When the forensic team has finished, I want you to go and see if there is anything missing."

CHAPTER 5:

THE MYSTERY ASSAILANT

Melissa walked through the wood. The boy following her kept pace with her – as he made sure Melissa could not sense him following her. He knew she had keen senses and could feel someone close to her – so he kept his distance. She listened to the sounds of the wood around her.

Melissa heard a sound close to her. She stopped and looked around, searching for whatever made the sound she heard.

He was quiet, holding his breath – waiting to see what Melissa would do next.

Melissa started moving through the wood again. He went towards her – he grabbed her from behind and held her against a tree. Melissa could not move her head, so she could not see who had grabbed her.

"Keep still, I'm not going to harm you."

"What do you want?"

A horrible thought came to her. "Did you kill my mother?"

"It would not be very good for you if I had."

"Do I take that as a no?"

The man laughed. "Of course – I have no reason to kill your mother."

There came the sound of movement from the other side of the cottage – he released her and disappeared into the cover of the trees. Melissa moved away from the tree she had been held against and walked across the overgrown back garden of the derelict cottage. Brendan Goodman came out from behind a tree. "Hi Mel, what have you been up to?"

"If I told you, I'd have to kill you."

Brendan smiled and shook his head.

"You shouldn't be saying things like that – or I would think you killed Brian Scott," Brendan said, seriously.

"I haven't killed anyone," Melissa said.

"Neither have I," Brendan said.

"Then why are you so secretive?" she inquired.

"There are things I can't tell you now. I want to find the killer of your mother as much as you do. It is possible she was killed because of the research we were working on. I could be next on the killer's list; Tabitha and Susan could also be in danger," Brendan explained.

Melissa stared at him. She realised she had not thought of that. Brendan took a decision and kissed her on the lips.

"Who was that you were talking to?"

Melissa stopped walking and stared at him.

"I don't know; he did not tell me his name."

"That's a pity – you know, you must be careful – your father is missing, and your mother was murdered. Did you recognise the voice?"

Melissa shook her head. Brendan put his arms round her and kissed her on the lips.

"It's about time we got to know each other better," he said.

Melissa put her arms round his neck and kissed him back.

"How do you know my father is missing?" she asked.

"David told me. That is why I was working with your mother – now it is my job to carry on with her work," Brendan said.

"You are very secretive about your past life – why do you want to tell me about yourself now?" she inquired.

Melissa moved away from him and walked out of the tree line and crossed the field that would take her to the Cook's farm. Brendan followed behind her.

"The killing of your mother is reason enough – I don't want you thinking I killed her."

They walked on in silence. They left the farm and walked up the path that led them to the cliff top installation. Melissa went to the living quarters. When she got there, she knocked on the door of the one Celeste and Nigel Barnet stayed in. Celeste opened the door and let her in.

"I saw you with Brendan," she accused.

Melissa smiled. "He wants to get to know me better."

"That's because he fancies you," Nigel Barnet said.

Melissa laughed. "Brendan's not the only one."

Celeste made coffee while Melissa and Nigel sat on the couch.

"Brendan and Keith are top of my list of suspects for the murders," Nigel said.

"It wasn't Brendan – I'm sure. I think I met the man who killed Brian in the wood, though. Brendan was close by listening – though he did not see his face." Celeste came in and handed out the mugs of coffee and sat on the other side of Melissa.

"I expect a lot of people here have skeletons hidden in their cupboards," Celeste said.

"Or buried in the woods somewhere," Melissa said.

Her two friends nodded in agreement.

CHAPTER 6:

THE DNA COLLECTERS

Rosalind Taylor was sitting in the kitchen drinking coffee. Donald Eastham and Celeste Barnet were there taking DNA and blood samples from Rosalind.

"What's all this about?" she asked.

"Nothing to be alarmed about, we are doing it to a lot of people in the area," Donald told her.

"You'll have to tell my father about your findings – he thinks I am not his daughter," Rosalind said.

"Why is that, Ros?" Celeste inquired.

"Look at me – I am slightly different to my parents," she said.

Celeste stared at her and noticed for the first time that Rosalind's eyes were grey with flecks of lilac in them. Her skin was very pale and almost translucent – her hair was dark with a purple sheen.

"I'll come and give you the results, we can certainly tell your father you are his daughter," Celeste said.

"Thank you," Rosalind said.

Donald and Celeste left the cottage and Rosalind went up to her room and lay on the bed and stared up at the ceiling and got down to some serious thinking.

Donald and Celeste returned to the Installation and entered the genetics laboratory building. They had been collecting DNA samples all over the surrounding area and Rosalind's was the most remarkable so far.

Donald was going to research the girl thoroughly to discover where her differences came from. The other members of his team were Nigel and Celeste Barnet – the brother-sister partnership worked well with him – sometimes Melissa would join them as she was the floater in the Installation.

AUGUST 2111

Melissa Davis came out of the main building and gazed at the large dark green armoured van parked by the main doors. Brendan was there talking to another man. She stood and watched them. After a while Brendan walked away, and Melissa ran up to the man.

"How well do you know Brendan?" she asked.

"More than I know you, young lady," he said.

Melissa smiled and told him her name. His expression turned serious.

"Brendan told me about you, I'm sorry for your loss."

"Thank you. Perhaps you can tell me about Brendan," she said.

"What do you want to know?"

"Brendan is very secretive about himself – it's very suspicious now there have been two murders here," Melissa explained.

The man smiled at her. "Brendan studies people – he does not kill them. I'm afraid he finds it more interesting discovering things about the people he works with, than talking about himself."

A tall young lady came out of the cab of the van. "Who's your friend, Dave?"

Melissa studied her – she had long brown hair and hazel eyes, she wore a black blazer and matching skirt.

The man smiled at her.

"This is Melissa. She was wondering if Brendan could have killed Brian Scott."

The young woman looked Melissa up and down. "They are bringing up the scientists younger these days."

Melissa glared at her. "I'm here because of my intelligence, not my age."

The man laughed. "She's got you there, Trace."

Tracy Morgan smiled and nodded her head to her. "When Brian disappeared, Brendan was working with me."

"Thank you. I don't want him to be guilty – I just want to know more about him."

David Walker and Tracy Morgan walked towards the mushroom structure. Melissa made for the central main building.

When she got through the entrance doors, she found Brendan waiting for her.

"Did you find out what you wanted?" he asked.

Melissa nodded. "The young woman told me you were working with her, when Brian disappeared."

"That's Tracy Morgan – she drives her van round the country visiting secret establishments," Brendan said.

"And the man?" she asked.

"David Walker – he sometimes joins her."

"He says you are more interested in finding out about other people than telling people about yourself," Melissa said.

Brendan put a hand on her chin and raised her head slightly and kissed her on the lips.

"You can cross me off your list now," he said – then he walked away.

Nigel Barnet was looking down a microscope. Celeste stood beside him.

Donald Eastham came over to them. "How's it going?"

Nigel got up. "Very interesting – have a look."

Donald looked down the microscope and after a few minutes he stood up.

"We'd better go and visit Rosalind," Celeste said.

Rosalind Taylor was with Janet Hodgson – she was keeping out of her father's way – she was sure he wanted to murder her. She wore a green and white striped dress. They were sitting on a low wall at the front of the cottage. A car drove down the track and parked close by. Donald and Celeste got out of the car and approached the three teenagers on the wall. Donald and Celeste told them the results of the blood tests.

"I hope they can convince my father I am his biological daughter," Rosalind said.

"Is there any reason he doesn't think you are his daughter?" Donald asked.

"Where do I start? My hair is different, my eyes are the wrong colour for him, my skin complexion is strange – in fact he thinks everything about me is strange to him," she said in a cold, angry voice. "Is that why you stay away from home so much?" Janet asked.

Rosalind nodded. "He'll kill me if I stay at home too much."

"What is the thing inside me that makes my father want to kill me?" she inquired.

"What about some sort of virus?" Janet queried.

Donald and Celeste exchanged glances. He told Rosalind there was some strange DNA in her that they had not seen before.

"Do you think it's alien DNA?" Rosalind inquired.

"Something was added to the gene pool – we are going to research it thoroughly," Donald said.

CHAPTER 7:

HELEN EASTHAM

OCTOBER 2111

Jeremy and Janet Hodgson left their cottage and walked out of the tree line. They followed the track that went around the farm and headed for the road. They saw a car parked at the entrance to Cook's Farm. A tall slim young woman got out – she wore a cream coloured blazer and skirt. Jeremy and Janet approached her.

"If you are going for a walk in the woods, you'll have to watch out – they're not kind to strangers," Jeremy said.

Helen Eastham smiled. "Is that so, they were all right to me, the last time I was here."

"We're always walking through the woods – we haven't seen you before," Janet said.

"I'm Helen Eastham-- it's nice to meet the both of you."

"I'm Janet Hodgson, I'm fourteen. This is my brother Jeremy – he's sixteen."

"Are you related to Donald Eastham?" Jeremy inquired.

Helen nodded. "I'm his sister."

Jeremy pointed to the high cliffs – Helen saw the installation sitting on top of them.

"Donald works up there," Jeremy said.

"Thanks," Helen said.

Helen got in her car and drove away. Jeremy and Janet walked down the path that led to the large farmhouse. They helped Brenda Cook with the feeding of the animals.

Helen drove up the track that led to the Installation. At the main gates a security guard came out to her and Helen showed her pass; which allowed her into every secret establishment in the country. He gave her back the pass and waved to his partner on the other side of the gates. They slid open and she drove onto the compound. She drove to the large central single-storey building and parked her car. She entered the building and walked along the corridor until she reached the offices and walked in. She had met Dr Elizabeth Wilkinson before, and they shook hands. They left the main building and crossed over to the genetics research building.

They entered the laboratory. Celeste and Nigel Barnet stood up from their work. Dr Wilkinson introduced them to Helen. Dr Wilkinson told Helen that Donald and his team had been taking DNA samples of the people living in the area and they were getting some interesting results. Donald came into the laboratory and hugged his sister – he was glad to see her. He told her about Rosalind Taylor, an interesting subject for his research.

"We've had a couple of murders," Donald said.

Dr Wilkinson and Helen left the building; Celeste and Nigel got on with their work.

"I have someone you should meet."

CHAPTER 8:

THE SENSITIVE

Melissa Davis and Adam Williams were having breakfast at her quarters. Her close companions were staying near to her to keep her safe. They were wondering if the two murders were connected and committed by the same killer. Adam and Nigel had questioned her about the mystery man in the woods who had grabbed her, but she could not give them anything that could identify the person. After they had finished breakfast Melissa went and stood by the window of her quarters and watched Dr Wilkinson and a striking young woman walk towards them. Adam came and stood behind her.

"We have visitors," Melissa said.

"I wonder what they want."

"We'll soon find out," Melissa said.

Melissa turned around and he kissed her on the lips – then she went to the door and opened it. She stood aside and let the two women in. She gazed at the newcomer – she liked the strong features of the pretty face and the intelligent blue-grey eyes.

"This is Donald's sister Helen. Melissa."

"Hello Melissa – it's nice to meet you."

"Donald is very proud of you – he talked a lot about you."

Melissa walked over to the couch and the others followed. Adam sat on an armchair. He looked at Helen.

"Donald told us you were an investigative journalist – that must be very interesting work," Adam said.

Helen smiled at him and nodded. "The case I am on now is very interesting," she said.Melissa gazed at Helen with wide bright brown eyes. "Has it anything to do with the murders here?"

"No – though I had to come here to learn more about them. There have been several strange disappearances – your father included; that is what I am investigating this minute," Helen explained.

Melissa sat up as her heart missed a beat – her mother had told Melissa her father had gone missing while working for the Government.

"I have still to learn what my mother and father were investigating," Melissa said.

"Dr Wilkinson says you are a sensitive – you should question Brendan about your mother's work and I'm sure Dr Wilkinson will help you with that. While I'm here, I could use your insight," Helen said.

"Of course – I'll do all I can to help," Melissa said.

"I've been to see DI Hunter and he told me about the death of your mother – I'm very sorry for your loss," Helen said.

"The killer who killed Brian Scott caught me in the woods. Luckily Brendan Goodman came along, and the killer ran amongst the trees – none of us saw his face," Melissa said.

Melissa and Adam exchanged glances then Melissa turned back to Helen.

"Do you know Brendan well?" Melissa asked.

"Yes, I've met him a few times," Helen replied.

"Do you think he could kill anyone?" Adam asked.

Helen shook her head. "Brendan is one of those people who can get what they want without running over or killing people."

Melissa turned to Adam. "We can cross him off our list," she said.

Helen stared at her. "You have a list?"

"We made up a list of likely candidates for the murders – we weren't going accuse anyone," Melissa said.

"That's sensible – if the killer thinks you are going after him, he may come after you," warned Helen.

Helen and Dr Wilkinson left the quarters. Adam got up and approached the couch and sat next to Melissa.

"Donald's sister is a smart young lady," Adam said.

Melissa grinned at him. "Keep your eyes off her – Helen is well out of your league."

Adam smiled and kissed her on the lips. "You are more in my league."

Adam got up and left the quarters. A few moments later, there came another knock on the door. Melissa opened the door and Brendan Goodman pushed past her and strode in.

"Don't you wait to be let in before barging in?" Melissa complained.

"I wanted to know why Helen visited you."

Melissa glared at him. "What do you think she wanted to know?"

"You might tell her you suspect me of murdering your mother," Brendan said, seriously.

"Helen told me you were a person who got what he wanted without killing people."

Brendan smiled. "I hope that makes you distrust me less."

"Your friend Tracy Morgan told me you did some work for her – what was that?"

"She came to me about a person I may help her with."

Melissa kept her eyes on his face. "Who was that?"

"Perhaps I can't tell you," Brendan said.

Melissa was not to be put off. "I want to know the people you associate with."

"Adrian Simpson."

Melissa's expression changed.

"Have you heard of him?" Brendan inquired.

Melissa nodded. "He attended my school. He used to tell everyone who would listen there was going to be a revolution."

"Tracy and her friend would be interested in that," Brendan said.

Brendan stood up and left the quarters.

Keith Watson entered Dr Wilkinson's office. He showed surprise when he saw Helen Eastham. He knew her by reputation and had followed her career with deep interest.

"Donald talked about you a lot – it's good to meet you at last."Helen smiled and asked Keith what he knew about the two murders.

"The same as everyone else – Brian disappeared, then sometime later Melissa found the spot where someone had buried him. Brian worked in Marina Davis's laboratory – that may be a reason she was targeted."

"Perhaps they saw something they shouldn't have," Helen said.

Keith nodded. "Everyone here has their agendas – anything is possible."

Helen exchanged glances with Dr Wilkinson and wondered what his agenda was.

"The killer may have been after Mel – but unfortunately her mother got in the way."

"Why Melissa?" Dr Wilkinson said.

Keith shrugged his shoulders. "Melissa has been doing some strange things lately and she's been playing the amateur detective."

"I've warned her about that," Helen said.

Keith walked out of the room and Dr Wilkinson gazed at Helen.

"Amateur detective is a dangerous occupation."

"Melissa wants to know who killed her mother," Helen said.

CHAPTER 9:

THE RAGE

The bursting pain inside Bruce Taylor's head was about to explode – it had been building up over the last month. Something was eating away at him inside the head – he had his own ideas as to the cause of it. He raced into the kitchen and his wife saw the fire in his bloodshot eyes.

Rosalind Taylor came in by the front door, all her senses alert for any danger. She walked along the hallway. The kitchen door was open, and she saw her mother lying on the kitchen floor. Bruce Taylor was standing over her. He suddenly looked up and turned – he saw the subject of his troubles. The staring grey eyes with the lilac flecks in them; the pale complexion – he was sure he had not helped to give birth to her – Rosalind was a pariah. She saw the hate and murder in his expression. She was aware he wanted to murder her.

Rosalind turned and dashed for the door – luckily, she had left the door open. She heard Bruce Taylor leap out of the kitchen. She ran out of the house and closed the door behind her. Rosalind ran into the trees as the door opened – she heard pursuit. She made her way through the wood for a short distance and dived down amongst a large clump of ferns. She kept still and quiet as she heard Bruce move through the wood close by. She heard him move off away from her; when she could hear him no longer, she stood up and raced out of the wood.

Rosalind ran onto the road and saw a car moving towards her; Rosalind waved it down. The car stopped, and the driver wound down the window. Rosalind told the driver a killer was after her. She turned and gazed at the tree line and saw Bruce Taylor rushing out. The rear door opened, and a tall girl got out and told her to get in the car.

Rosalind got in the back of the car and the tall girl sat beside her and slammed the door.

David Walker stared at the man running towards the car, wondering whether to get out and have a word with him or drive off. He gazed at the crazed red eyes and foaming mouth and he decided not to go anywhere near him. David started the car and drove off.

"He's doesn't look like a man who will listen to reason," he said.

David took a left turning and drove past the village. Rosalind had an idea where he was going, and she looked at the tall girl.

"I'm Rosalind, you are going to the cliff top Installation?"

She nodded. "I'm Patricia – David wants me to meet some of the scientists working there."

Detective Sergeant Martin Sanderson drove up the track – that was just wide enough for his car. It led him into the trees and to the cottage where the murder was reported to have taken place. PC Rachel Robertson was sitting in the passenger seat beside him. He parked the car in front of the cottage – the front door was open. They got out of the car and walked into the hallway of the cottage. PC Robertson called out – but only silence greeted her call. DS Sanderson walked to the kitchen door which was closed. He opened the door and stared down at the dead woman. PC Robertson took out her mobile phone and called the pathology lab and spoke to Dr John Walsh.

She went upstairs and checked the rooms – she found a photograph of Rosalind and went downstairs and showed it to Martin.

"That's the daughter," she said.

"I hope she was able to get away," DS Sanderson said.

"I'll go outside and have a look round."

"Shout out if you see Bruce Taylor," Martin said. Dr John Walsh and the forensic team entered the cottage and got down to work. DS Sanderson stood still and watched the pathologist as he studied the body.

"It was a very frenzied attack," Dr Walsh said.

"There seems to be a lot of them lately."

John Walsh looked up at him. "The medical research people are considering it."

"Considering what?"

DS Sanderson turned and watched DI Hunter walk into the kitchen. PC Robertson walked up to the tree line. There was a rustling in the undergrowth – Rachel got ready for trouble. A teenage boy and girl stepped out of the tree line.

"Did you see anyone in the woods?"

The girl smiled at her. "We saw Bruce Taylor rushing through the trees; we came to see if Rosalind was all right."

"The girl's not here now," Rachel said.

DS Sanderson came out to join them.

"Rosalind told us Bruce Taylor wanted to kill her," Jeremy said.

"We saw him running through the woods," Janet said.

"Where in the woods did you see him?" DS Sanderson asked.

"We'll show you," Jeremy said.

They walked through the tree line and the two teenagers stood still.

"He ran off into the woods here," Janet said.

DS Sanderson told them to run off home and leave Bruce Taylor to the police. He watched the two teenagers disappear further into the woods – then DS Sanderson found Bruce Taylor lying on the ground. He picked up a limp wrist and felt for a pulse but found none. He turned to Rachel and shook his head. He took out his mobile phone and informed DI Hunter of what they had found, and he told them to stay there and wait for the forensic team.

Sometime later Dr Moira Banks and Brendan Goodman entered the cottage. She told DS Sanderson that John Walsh had called her to pick up the body and take it to the installation mortuary. Bruce Taylor was put in a body bag and Brendan zipped it up.

Bruce Taylor lay on a slab in the mortuary. Dr Moira Banks started the autopsy. Dr Emily Stuart watched the proceedings – she had taken the place of Marina Davis. David Walker stood beside her. They were both very interested in the findings of what had driven the man to murder his wife and chase after his daughter to do the same to her.

Dr Moira Banks knew the answer to Bruce Taylor's problems was inside his skull. She shaved it and sawed off the top of the skull – to her horror, a sliding mass of organic matter moved slowly out of the brain case. David and Emily moved closer to the table.

"That's the worst we've had yet," David said.

The two women stared at him.

Patricia Evans got up from the desk computer when David and Dr Stuart entered the office. She stared at David and shook her head. Brendan Goodman stood by the window and David told him the state of Bruce Taylor's brain.

"What do we do now?" Brendan inquired.David smiled at him. "I'm going to see your friend Melissa."

David turned to Patricia and asked her to see how Rosalind was getting on – she was having a complete medical check-up.

The mortuary assistant walked into the laundry and took her mobile phone out of her pocket and dialled the number. A man's voice answered. "There's been another one," she said.

Dr Brian Stonehouse listened to the woman's voice on the phone as she told him about Bruce Taylor – who had killed his wife in a rage and then died of something that turned his brain into mush.

The loud rap on the door made Melissa jump and she nearly spilt her coffee. She opened the door and smiled when she saw David Walker.

"Can I come in?" he asked.

Melissa stood aside and let him in, then closed the door behind him.

"Do you know what my father was doing before he disappeared?" Melissa demanded.

David nodded and told her about the death of Bruce Taylor and how they were investigating the brain destroying organism that killed him. They had lost contact with Melissa's father – who was trying to discover where it had originated.

"Brendan was working with your mother on the project – you have no reason to fear him," David said.

Melissa smiled and told David she had already decided that herself.

"I'd like to have a look at your mother's computer, to see if there is anything for me on it, or if anything has been taken from it," David said. Melissa looked at him in surprise.

"Whatever for?" she asked.

"I want to see if there is anything there for me on it," David said.

"You did not tell me you knew my mother when we first met."

David smiled and nodded. "Yes – I should have asked you then."

Melissa guided him to her mother's study.

"Are you trying to find who killed her?"

"You could say that," he said.

Melissa stood by the desk and activated the computer. "My mother got a call before she was killed – we never found out who it was."

"You don't have to worry about that – it was me – we were working on something together," David said.

Melissa stared at him and wondered what other surprises he had for her. She went through the data on the computer – there was nothing about what she had been working on.

"Did you find anything missing?" David asked.

"DI Hunter asked me that. I had a good look round, but I could not find anything out of place," Melissa said.

"How are you bearing up?"

Melissa smiled. "I'm kept busy."

"I met your father as well as your mother – protecting you has fallen to me," David said, sincerely.

"Do you think the person who killed Mother had something to do with my father's disappearance?"

"It's a possibility – I don't want anything bad to happen to you."

CHAPTER 10:

THE BACTERIOLOGICAL LABORATORY

JANUARY 2112

Patricia Evans and Sheila Watkins walked up the track that led to two large cottages. Patricia looked towards the left-hand cottage – there was a large black car parked out front with dark tinted windows. Sheila opened the front door and turned to see what Patricia was up to.

"What's up, Pat?"

Patricia turned and gazed at her friend.

"Does your friend drive a car like that?" Sheila asked.

Patricia shook her head and walked into the cottage. Sheila followed behind her and shut the front door.

"A person driving a car like that has something to hide."

Patricia nodded in agreement. "That's what I mean."

They went into the kitchen and Sheila opened the back door, then turned to her friend.

"It's a wonder your father doesn't drive around in a car like that," Sheila said.

Patricia smiled – her father was a security agent for large industrial companies.

"Who used to live in this cottage?" Patricia asked.

"A woman and her daughter – they both disappeared."

"Let's hope we don't disappear," Patricia said.

"We are not here to disappear," assured Sheila.

Sheila stepped outside and looked around; she gazed across at the other cottage. Inside it a man was watching her – he turned to his companion; who owned the cottage.

"You have a new neighbour."

The tall man in a dark suit came and stood beside his companion.

They watched the second girl exit the cottage. Matthew smiled and turned to his companion.

"Pat seems to be following you about."

"She is trying to follow in her father's footsteps, Matthew."

"More likely, she is just plain nosey," Matthew said.

FEBRUARY 2112

Patricia Evans and Sheila Watkins were having lunch with Matthew, the next-door neighbour; he did not offer a surname. David Walker wanted to know more about the man and Patricia was working on it. She saw his companion sometimes, but she did not see his face clearly. After lunch the two girls left the cottage.

David Walker drove up the track and parked the car in front of the right-hand cottage. Patricia gazed across at the other cottage. The large dark car with the tinted windows was there. A man in a dark suit wearing dark glasses came out of the cottage and got into the car.

"He looks a shifty guy," David said.

They watched the car drive down the track towards the road.

"I can't find out much about the man – the car is owned by the agency," David said.

"Perhaps he is part of the Installation security people," Patricia said.

David nodded and decided to find out if he was.

David drove to the Installation and parked his car and saw Melissa Davis heading for the Bio Lab. He raced after her.

"Hello Mel – are you working with Dr Stuart today?" he inquired.

Melissa nodded. "It's nice to see what Mother was working on," she said.

They entered the building and went to the locker room and picked up a white lab coat each and then went to the laboratory. Melissa spied Dr Stuart looking at an electron microscope – she went to the woman to announce her arrival.

"What's in there – a bug?" Melissa inquired.

Emily nodded. "That's what drove Bruce Taylor mad."

"I suppose you are going to say it is not of this Earth," Melissa wondered.

Dr Stuart grinned at her. "How did you guess?"

Melissa gazed at David – as he probably had more information about the subject.

"We have an extra-terrestrial microbe – that drove Bruce Taylor mad and imploded his brains," David said.

"Are we going to have an epidemic?" Melissa inquired.

"Not here – it has a short life and died with Bruce; Rosalind and her mother did not have it. I'm sure your mother discovered something – perhaps the killer stole her data."

"I didn't find anything on my computer or my mother's. Brendan told me you were interested in Adrian Simpson – he attended the same school as me – could he know someone here who could steal information for him?"

"That's interesting, Mel – we'll consider it," David said.

David was very impressed with Melissa – there was a lot of her mother and father in her thinking. He left the quarters and drove out of the Installation.

Dr Emily Stuart took Melissa in hand and told her about the research they were doing – she told Melissa she had worked with both of her parents and they were a great loss to the scientific community. She was very sorry for Melissa losing both her parents and Emily assured the girl she would give her guidance and all the help she needed.

Melissa thanked her and told Dr Stuart she was thrilled to be working with her. She gazed across the laboratory. Susan Bishop and Tabitha Dawson gave her the thumbs up – as they were glad Melissa was working with them.

CHAPTER 11:

ISABEL THE REBEL

MARCH 2112

Isabel Eastham stood at the bedroom window and stared out at her new surroundings. Isabel and her sick mother had taken over Rosalind's cottage – she had been uprooted from her home in the big city and deposited in the country, away from her studies and university. Her father had died the month before, then her mother moved them down to the country, and then her mother got ill, and Isabel was tied down to the cottage. The career Isabel had planned was now on hold. Isabel had to limit her studies to her bedroom and the desk computer. This was the first time Isabel had been in the country – she was a city girl at heart. She gazed across the back garden and thought about the dark woodland beyond; she was determined to keep away from it – in case there were wild animals living in it.

Isabel was eighteen, just over six feet and had a full curvy figure, she had short brown hair and bright hazel eyes. Isabel was sure she was going to be somebody one day – if the world let her. She was intelligent and clever, and Isabel had plans she wanted to put into action. Her lecturers at university were very praiseworthy of the knowledge and application she showed to her chosen science subject. Some of her ideas were controversial – but she had no problem with that. Isabel was a girl who loved to find new avenues to follow in her science and fight the ethics and morals that were attached to it. Isabel knew she would achieve her goal – it was just a matter of time.

Isabel left her bedroom and visited her mother, who did not want anything, so she left the room and walked out of the cottage.

Isabel walked up the track and turned left and walked along the side of the road. She eventually came to a left turn – which she took – the village was on her right on the other side of the road. She came to a farm and a tall, slim girl was moving out of the entrance to the farm – she gave Isabel a smile.

"You are the newcomer?"

Isabel nodded and told the girl her name.

"I'm Janet – it's good to meet you. Do you know Donald and Helen Eastham?"

"Yes – they are my cousins," Isabel replied.

"I'm Janet Hodgson – I hope we can be good friends."

"I don't see why not – I need some new friends," Isabel said.

Janet walked towards the woods and after a moment's thought Isabel followed her into the tree line. They walked through the wood, until Adam Williams came upon them.

"Where did you spring from?" Janet asked.

Adam Williams smiled at her and gazed at Isabel – Janet explained who her new friend was. Adam asked her what work she did. Isabel told them she was still at university and was hoping to be a scientist. Adam told her about the cliff top Installation, telling her it was a scientific establishment. Isabel told him that Donald was her cousin and asked who was in charge.

"Dr Elizabeth Wilkinson," Adam said.

Isabel had heard of her and she wondered if Helen could get her an interview with the head scientist.

Adam told Janet, he was going to the other side of the wood, to check on a cottage there. Janet knew the one he meant.

"The boy who lives there keeps watching me, when I am in the woods with Jeremy."

"Melissa and I have caught a sight of him, he might have killed Brian Scott," Adam said.

The two girls followed Adam through the wood, until they arrived at their destination. Janet and Isabel watched Adam run up the overgrown path to the back door of the old cottage – the two girls stared after him.

Janet watched him enter the cottage, then turned to Isabel who shrugged her shoulders. Janet ran up the path, Isabel followed her and they passed through the kitchen and went into the hallway. Adam stood at the cellar door, then he made his way down the stone steps. Janet walked to the cellar door. Isabel stood in the kitchen doorway, wondering what Janet and her friend were up to.

"It looks as if nobody has lived here for decades," Isabel said.

Janet turned to her. "Only the ghosts live here now."

Isabel hoped Janet was joking. She asked her new friend if she had seen a ghost but Janet shook her head.

"I've seen a few strange things in the wood, but I haven't seen a ghost – though I know someone who has," Janet said.

Janet made her way down the stone steps and Isabel followed behind her. A shaft of light came from a broken window high up the rear wall of the cellar.

Adam Williams stood at the side of an old wardrobe, against the rear wall. He saw a pair of bare feet on the floor sticking out from behind the wardrobe. He asked Janet to give him a hand to move the wardrobe, so they could see what was behind it. There was a body of a teenage girl, in a lime green bikini – lying behind the wardrobe. Adam told Janet to leave the cottage with Isabel and contact the police.

Janet contacted the police on her mobile phone and then told Isabel to go back home. "Adam and I will talk to the police," Janet said.

DI Hunter studied the two faces before him, as he listened to their statements on how they had found the girl's body. The forensic team were in the cellar. Janet told DI Hunter who the girl was, as she knew her. He remembered soon after Suzanne disappeared, her mother went missing soon after. He turned his attention on Adam Williams – he knew the boy worked with Melissa in the Installation.

"You seem to be taking it in turns with Melissa, in finding dead bodies."

"It seems that way."

Hunter turned to the girl. "Do you come to this cottage often?"

"Sometimes," Janet replied.

DI Hunter told them to keep away from the old cottage. Then he left them and entered the cottage and went down to the cellar. DS Sanderson stood by the wardrobe while forensic pathologist John Walsh studied the body. He told Hunter a broken neck had killed the girl – quick and professional.

When Isabel got home, she made some tea and took a cup up to her mother. Isabel told her she had been out for a walk. She placed the cup on the bedside table. Margaret Eastham stared at Isabel, without saying anything. Isabel left the room and went to her bedroom to drink her tea; when she had drunk it she went downstairs to fix lunch. A few moments later the doorbell rang. She opened the door and found her cousin Helen standing on the doorstep. They went into the kitchen.

"You've come just in time – I was just fixing lunch," Isabel said.

"I'm sorry I have not looked in till now – I was sorry to hear about your father," Helen said.

Helen went up to see Margaret – who was happy to see her. When Helen came back to the kitchen, Isabel was dishing out lunch.

"Do you know a Dr Elizabeth Wilkinson?"

Helen nodded, and Isabel told her cousin she had met Janet Hodgson who had told her that Dr Wilkinson was the head scientist in a cliff top scientific installation.

"Perhaps you could tell her about me and the science I want to be involved in," Isabel said.

"I have been keeping up with your achievements at university – I'm sure she would be interested in your work," Helen said.

"I have a career to pursue," Isabel said.

"Until I can get someone to look after your mother, you are stuck here I'm afraid, but I'll certainly help you get back on track with your studies."

"I trust you, Helen – more than anyone," Isabel said.

"I shall never betray that trust," Helen promised, sincerely.

At midnight Melissa got out of bed and put on a black sweatshirt, and black slacks, she left the quarters and went to the security shed. The guard on duty was Ben Welkin who looked at her in surprise.

"Hello Melissa, you are up late," he said.

Melissa sat on the side of the desk. "I want you to do something for me," she said.

"What is that?"

"I want you to let me out the main gate," Melissa said.

Ben shook his head. "It is not allowed this time of night."

Melissa nodded. "I know, but I want try something, I won't be long, I shall contact you on my mobile, when I am on my way back."

They left the security hut and went to the main gate, he let her out and shut the gate. Melissa ran down the slope and ran into the tree line; she went past the Hodgson cottage and went deeper into the woods. She wondered if the boy that lurked in the wood was somewhere near keeping pace with her. A dead girl had been found in his cottage; he was dangerous. Melissa stopped and listened, but only the usual sounds of the wood came to her ears. Melissa turned and went back the way she had come. Melissa returned to the Installation, and the guard let her in.

CHAPTER 12:

DEATH IN THE WOODS

Melissa Davis was making her way through the wood; she had been glad David had turned up for her sixteenth birthday – showing he cared what happened to her. She told him how she was getting on working with Dr Emily Stuart and Brendan. Melissa stared about her, as she walked through the woods – she searched and ducked down into the undergrowth. The sound faded away and she stood up and moved away and came upon one of the paths that ran through the wood.

He dumped the body on the path. He had seen Melissa lurking in the woods – she seemed to appear from nowhere. The girl was up to something and he would have to find out what – he did not want to kill her as he wanted to use her for his own ends. He hoped she would find the body – he decided not to bury her – like he did to Brian Scott – it would give Melissa something to think about. He moved into the trees and waited – then Melissa came into view.

Melissa moved along the path, stopping on occasions, and gazing about her, as she imagined many eyes watching her from the depths of the wood. Something was drawing her senses to this part of the wood – something strong and primeval.

She shivered even though it was humid in the wood. She was sure there was someone near watching her. She wore a green t-shirt and brown skirt – she hoped it would help her blend into the hues of the wood. She kept moving along the path and eventually she came to the body. Melissa put a hand to her mouth to stifle a scream. It was Dr Elizabeth Wilkinson – Melissa could not think why she had been in the woods and wondered if her body had been dumped here and she had been killed elsewhere.

Melissa suddenly got the feeling that someone was close by – she scanned the trees on both sides of the path.

"Who's there?" she called out.

A few moments later someone came up behind Melissa and grabbed her arm. She spun round and glared at Brendan Goodman.

"What are you up to?" Melissa inquired, sharply.

Brendan let go of her arm and stared down at the body on the path.

"When I learnt that Dr Wilkinson had left the compound I went to see if I could find her. Finding no information about her whereabouts, I also knew you were nowhere to be found, so I went into the woods to see if I could find you," Brendan explained.

Brendan took out his mobile phone and contacted the police. Melissa moved away from him and stepped into the wood. She took a deep breath and took in the odours of the dense wood. She concentrated on the sounds her sharp hearing could pick up on. Melissa heard someone, or something, moving away from her and deeper into the wood. She moved back onto the path.

"Did you sense anything?" Brendan asked.

Melissa nodded. "Someone was lurking close by – probably the killer."

"You don't think it's me? That's a relief," Brendan said.

Melissa smiled. "I think the body was dumped here and killed elsewhere; they probably hoped I would find it."

Brendan smiled at her. "What do you think, hoping you might be accused of killing her – or just to give you something to think about?"

Melissa was amazed at his thinking and thought he had a point.

"We'll have to find out where Dr Wilkinson went after she left the installation," Melissa said.

Melissa made her way down the path and Brendan stayed with the body. Eventually the path took her to the tree line. As she passed out of the wood the police vehicles were parking on the grass at the side of the road. Melissa stood still and watched DI Hunter and DS Sanderson approach her. When they got to her DS Sanderson asked her why bodies were being left around for her to find.

"The killer either wants me to be accused of the murders – or it's a message to say I might be next," Melissa informed him.

Melissa turned away from him and fell under the stern gaze of DI Hunter.

"I told your friend – you are taking it in turns to find a body."

Melissa gave him a puzzled expression as if she had no idea what he meant. He then told her that the day before Adam Williams had found the body of Abigail Waldron. Melissa had come back a day late.

"It's hot and sweaty in there," Melissa said, pointing to the wood.

Melissa took the path into the wood and the two police officers followed behind her.

"Do you know who the victim is?" DI Hunter asked.

"It was our head scientist; Dr Elizabeth Wilkinson."

"Have you any idea who killed her?" DS Sanderson asked.

Melissa shook her head. "I only know who didn't kill her."

Melissa guided them to the body. Brendan was still there waiting for the police. Melissa told them about how she found the body and Brendan had turned up a few moments later. Brendan told the police he had been looking for Melissa. He had not seen anyone else in the wood. Melissa told DI Hunter that she sensed someone was close, but she did not see them.

"I think she was killed elsewhere and dumped here," Melissa said.

"So, you could find her," Hunter said.

Melissa nodded. "The killer obviously has a thing for me."

"That's why you should not spend so much time alone, especially in the woods," Brendan said.

"Sounds like good advice, Mel," DI Hunter said.

Melissa nodded and said nothing – her mind was on overdrive.

"I can't think who would want to kill Dr Wilkinson," Brendan said.

Dr Walsh turned up and crouched down to study the body. DI Hunter told him who the victim was, and that she may have been dumped in the woods.

"It looks as if someone is getting rid of the opposition to their promotion bid," John Walsh said.

Brendan and Melissa stared at each other. DI Hunter asked them who would take over from Dr Wilkinson.

"Dr Emily Stuart will probably get the post – she is too busy to go about killing people," Brendan told him.

"Can you vouch for her?" DS Sanderson inquired.

Brendan nodded. "Absolutely. I work in her department, so does Melissa."

DI Hunter drove Brendan and Melissa back to the installation. Brendan took him to Dr Stewart Gilligan's office. He was very shocked to hear about Dr Wilkinson's death and had no idea who would want to kill her. Dr Gilligan told DI Hunter that Dr Emily Stuart would be taking over from the murdered scientist. Dr Gilligan showed him to the laboratory where Emily Stuart worked. When they walked into her office they found Brendan there – he had given her the bad news about Dr Wilkinson.

"I did not want to get promotion this way – Elizabeth was well liked," Emily told Dr Gilligan.

"That's the second time it's happened to you," DI Hunter said.

Emily Stuart stared at him. "I was unfortunately the best person to take over from Marina Davis. The Minister of Sciences would not have appointed me if I had homicidal tendencies."

DI Hunter smiled and nodded. "I suppose not. Thank you for your cooperation."

When DI Hunter and Dr Gilligan had left, Emily gazed at Brendan.

"I hope Melissa doesn't think the way the police do."

Brendan shook his head. "Mel knows you have nothing to do with her mother's death. I suppose it was a thought he had to bring up. I don't think he really believes you are involved with the two murders."

Melissa told Adam Williams about the murder of Dr Wilkinson – they were in her quarters – she told Adam she had learnt about the body he had found from the police.

"Somehow you are tied to the killer and you almost caught him dumping the body," Adam said.

"We both sense each other, so he was aware I was somewhere close," Melissa said.

"I hope the killer is caught soon before he goes after Dr Stuart," Adam said.

Adam left and a few moments later Brendan called on her and they went into the kitchen and Melissa made coffee for them both.

"You were right in what you said – about spending too much time alone in the woods," Melissa said.

They sat on the couch and sipped the coffee.

"I just want you to know I am no danger to you," Brendan said.

Melissa kissed him on the cheek. "I know."

Melissa sipped her coffee. "You are a watcher – have you seen anything worthwhile?"

Melissa had not come across the term – *the watcher* – but it fitted what he did – it applied to the killer as well.

"Not yet - but I'll tell you as soon as I do," Brendan said.

They finished their coffees and Brendan left the quarters.

Helen Eastham slid elegantly out of the shower. She dried her body and went to the bedroom and got dressed. She went downstairs as the doorbell rang. She opened the door and smiled at the man on the doorstep. Helen stood aside and let him in and closed the door behind him.

"Hello Douglas, I'm glad you could make it."

Douglas Heathcoat was the Minister of Science for the Government; she did some work for him. They went into the kitchen and Helen made some coffee. Douglas sat at the table and told Helen about the death of Dr Wilkinson – she turned and faced him. Donald told her Emily Stuart would be taking her place as head scientist.

"Who will be doing Marina Davis' research?"

"Dr Emily Stuart will still oversee that – it is her field," Douglas said.

Helen sat opposite Douglas and sipped her coffee.

"There is something you can do for me."

Helen had taken some print outs from Isabel's computer about the studies she was doing. Helen handed them to Douglas and told him what they were and hoped he would find them interesting.

"I have a lot of faith in my cousin Isabel – I hoped you could show them to someone who would be interested in her work," Helen said.

Douglas looked through the computer print outs and was impressed with the work of Helen's cousin and her ideas on a cloning programme.

"We've had reports from Dr Albert Harris about Isabel Eastham – he is very excited about her work and he ignored the wild child attitude of your cousin," Douglas said.

Helen smiled – she knew about the reports of Isabel being a bit of rebel.

"I'm trying to sort out that part of her character," Helen said.

"I know someone who will be very interested in your cousin's work," Douglas said.

When Douglas had left the cottage a few minutes later Isabel came back and introduced Helen to her new friend, Janet Hodgson. Helen told Isabel "someone from the Government is taking your work to show someone who will be very interested in it".

"You are so good to me," Isabel said.

"I am very proud of you, Isabel – I care for you a lot," Helen said, sincerely.

Helen left the cottage and made for the installation. Isabel took Janet to her bedroom. Isabel lay on her back on the bed and Janet sat on the edge of the bed. Isabel took a book off the bedside table and flipped through the pages.

"Is that a good book?" Janet asked.

"I'm still working on my studies – while I'm stuck here."

Janet studied the book. "You must be a brainy girl."

Isabel smiled and thanked her. "I'm studying genetics and cloning – people are concerned about the direction my studies are going."

"You must not give up in the face of adversity," Janet said. Isabel smiled – she liked Janet – she was a very sensible girl.

"Thank you for that, Janet – I've no intention of letting anyone stop me from getting what I want," Isabel said, defiantly.

Isabel got off the bed when her mother called. She went into the next bedroom to receive her mother's orders.

CHAPTER 13:

A SHOCK FOR ISABEL

When Isabel had done everything her mother wanted, she went and sat on the sill and gazed out of the window.

"I must be a very evil girl, Mother."

Isabel did not expect an answer and she did not get one. She turned away from the window.

"Can't you tell me why you hate me so much?"

Margaret Eastham turned to face her daughter.

"If you can't stand me, let me go," Isabel pleaded.

"I don't hate you – I just don't understand you."

Damn right.

Isabel walked to the bed and stared down at her mother's pale face. There was something not right about her mother's attitude towards her, that nagged at Isabel's mind. She knew it was nothing she had done; when Isabel was a small girl, she did everything she could to gain her mother's love – but Margaret always pushed her away; then when Isabel was a teenager, she gave up. At least her father had treated her with respect.

"Father could not understand why you disliked me so much."

Margaret stared at Isabel – the girl was a constant reminder of her past misdemeanour. Twenty years ago, her husband was away on business and she was lonely and bored. She had gone out to find someone she could have fun with. A tall dark stranger swept Margaret off her feet and turned her life upside down. She found him irresistible – as he stared at her with his hypnotic eyes. They had had a two month long tempestuous affair, which resulted in the conception of Isabel. "He wasn't your father," Margaret said.

Isabel stared at her mother in disbelief. "What are you telling me?"

"I had a lover when I was alone – you are the product of that union."

Isabel was stunned; it gave her the reason her mother was so cold to her, at least. Isabel felt humiliated and betrayed; she dashed out of the room. The anger burned inside her. Isabel rushed into her own room and dived onto her bed. Janet was sitting at the computer desk on the other side of the room. She stood up and went to the bed and sat on the edge of it.

"You came in here at a rate of knots – what's up, Isabel?"

Isabel kept silent and let her temper cool down. After a while she looked at Janet – the girl was looking at her in deep concern. Isabel told her what she had learnt from her mother about her father.

"No wonder you are so angry. I am here for you," Janet said.

Isabel slid off the bed. "Let's go downstairs and have some sweet strong coffee."

They went down to the kitchen and Isabel made some coffee, then they went into the lounge and sat on the couch.

"Your father must have loved you – you must not forget that."

Isabel was glad she had met Janet. "I won't."

They sipped their coffee as they went through their own private thoughts.

CHAPTER 14:

TYING UP LOOSE ENDS

Douglas Heathcoat drove his car through the main gate of the research facility on Exmoor. He drove to the medical research building; he parked the car and got out. He entered the building and went to Dr Richard Blake's office. Douglas handed him the computer printouts that Helen had given him.

"I thought someone here would be interested in that data."

Dr Blake read them and saw what the Minister of Science meant. After a while he looked up at Douglas.

"Very controversial," Dr Blake said.

"Isabel Eastham is a very controversial girl."

The two men left the office and walked down a long corridor and at the end they went through some double doors. They entered a large room with white walls and ceiling. They approached a tall, slender young woman in a white lab coat, with short blonde hair. She stood between two life support capsules; in each of them was a baby girl. One lay still with eyes closed – the other was wide awake, and the bright emerald green eyes stared out at the movement outside the glass case.

Dr Blake handed the computer printouts to the young woman who looked through them and the further she got through the data the more excited she got. Dr Blake stared down at the small ginger haired baby – the bright green eyes stared up at him. A small hand reached up and touched the glass top; a smile flickered over the thin lips.

"She likes you, Richard."

"We'd be happier if her twin sister showed signs of life," Dr Blake said.

The young woman silently agreed.

"You seem very interested in the data I brought you," Douglas Heathcoat said.

"I must meet the author of this remarkable research."

"I thought you would find it interesting – I'll set up an interview between the both of you," Douglas said.

"I would be very grateful," she said.

Isabel lay on her back on the bed gazing up at the ceiling; Janet Hodgson sat on the edge of the bed. Isabel had no idea of the roller coaster ride she was going on to achieve the destiny she craved. She was going to rush violently into a world of terror and discovery. She would never be the same girl again.

"Have you been here long enough to have a feeling something nasty is happening round here?" Janet asked.

Isabel smiled at her. "Finding a body in a cellar and finding out the man who brought me up wasn't my father. That tells me something is not right."

"I have to go – I'll see you later." Janet stood up and walked towards the door. Isabel got up and saw Janet out of the cottage.

Late in the evening Isabel opened the back door and stepped out; all was still and quiet. The sky was dark and overcast – she felt rain in the air. Lurking in the trees on her right was a tall dark figure; two amber eyes stared at her. He was surprised to see Margaret Eastham in the area, and she had a girl with her. A red tongue ran over thin lips – he had some loose ends to sort out.

Isabel turned and stared at the trees on her right – she could see something staring back at her – then it was gone. Isabel turned away and went back into the cottage. Something rammed into her back knocking her sprawling onto the kitchen floor. Isabel knew there was danger and her mind and body got ready for the fight for survival. A foot stamped down on the centre of her back and strong hands gripped her shoulders. The thumbs dug into her flesh seeking the pressure points; Isabel sudden felt her strength slowly ebb away; she started to feel weak. A few moments later he picked her up and carried her into the hallway, then up the stairs. When he was on the landing a woman called out the girl's name.

The mystery person kicked in the door and strode into the room. Margaret sat up in bed – she was shocked to see the tall dark stranger again. He laid Isabel across the bed.

"Hello Margaret – is this yours?"

"She is ours," Margaret said.

He stared down at the girl and knew that was why he was drawn to the girl. She was an item to be fully studied. Isabel tried to look up at her attacker as he held her down on the bed face down. In the gloomy light in the room she tried to make out the features; she got the impression of a tall thin figure, with claws and a mouth with long sharp teeth. She blinked as the two bright amber eyes stared down at her.

"You can certainly pick them, Mother," Isabel said.

He kept a grip on her, pressing his thumbs into the pressure points; keeping Isabel weak and malleable.

"I've come to tie up some loose ends."

Margaret stared at the amber eyes – one hand was moved away from Isabel and moved out of sight. He pulled a long silvery blade from his dark clothes. He looked menacingly at Margaret – there was nothing she could do about him; she was too weak and ill to fight him.

Isabel could not move as the assailant was immensely strong and kept her down on the bed. She was going to be forced to watch the murder of her mother. Then she would be next. The silvery blade was thrust into Margaret; Isabel was sprayed with blood. Isabel closed her eyes. When the assailant had finished with her mother, Isabel was pulled off the bed and dragged across the floor to the door. She was dragged along the landing and into her bedroom.

"You belong to me now."

Isabel stared at the amber eyes as they stared down at her – they bored into her brain; her mind screamed out as the silver blade was held up for her eyes to see.

Isabel closed her eyes and readied herself for the pain and humiliation that was to come to her body and mind.

CHAPTER 15:

TEETERING OVER THE EDGE OF MADNESS

In the morning Janet Hodgson cycled along the road until she got to the track she had to turn down. A large black car with tinted windows came up it and nearly knocked Janet off her bicycle.

"Somebody's in a hurry," she shouted after the car as it sped onto the road.

When she reached the old cottage, Janet hopped off her bicycle and went to the front door and rang the doorbell. After a while when she got no answer, Janet went around the back. As she turned the corner something grey and blurred came out of the open back door and made for the wood and disappeared into the trees. Janet knew something bad had happened in the cottage. She went into the kitchen and then went into the hallway. She called out to Isabel but got no answer. All was still and quiet. She went up the stairs and stood on the landing – both bedroom doors were open.

Janet went to Isabel's mother's room and stared in horror – the odour of blood assailed her nostrils. She left the room and went to Isabel's room, expecting the worst. She found Isabel on the bed – there was no movement. She ran a soothing hand over the girl's face.

"Speak to me, Isabel please," Janet said.

Janet heard the front door open and she rushed out of the room and stood at the top of the stairs. Helen Eastham stood in the hallway.

"Quick, Helen, Isabel's mother has been murdered and Isabel is in a bad way."

Helen ran up the stairs and looked in Margaret's room, then she took out her mobile phone and contacted the police. Then she went in to see Isabel.

Isabel opened her eyes and stared at Helen. "I didn't do it."

"We know you didn't do this awful thing," Helen said.

"I saw the killer leave the cottage by the back door," Janet said.

Helen stared at her and Janet told her what she had seen, and that she had seen the same thing in the woods some time ago.

"I never got a clear sight of it," Janet said.

Helen went downstairs to wait for the police whilst Janet stayed with Isabel. A few minutes later DS Sanderson came into the room.

"Death follows you about, Miss Hodgson."

"There's a homicidal maniac running amok in my back yard - it's not my fault," Janet complained.

"Let's hope we catch him before he comes after you."

Janet made a face at him. "Oh, thanks for that."

Sanderson smiled at her.

Janet told him what she had seen when she arrived at the cottage; she had no hopes that he would believe her.

"This killer is going to take some catching," Janet said.

"We'll put the flying squad on it," DS Sanderson said, seriously.

Janet giggled. "You'll need them."

DI Hunter was questioning Helen to see if she thought Isabel could have killed her mother. Helen shook her head.

"Isabel has her problems; but she would not kill anyone."

Helen told him about the mystery lover – who turned out to be Isabel's real father.

"Perhaps he came back and sorted things out," Helen said.

The forensic pathologist gave Hunter his report. It was a relief to Helen that he told them the evidence showed that Isabel was held over the bed, so she could witness her mother's murder. The murder weapon was a long sharp blade – the killer took his time before delivering the fatal stab. The paramedics had been in to see Isabel – who was still unconscious; there were bruises all over her body. Whoever it was did not want to kill her – just cause her immense pain and discomfort.

Janet sat on a chair at the bedside. She ran a hand over Isabel's forehead. Her tortured mind had fallen into a dark pit, where she was fighting for her sanity. Janet gazed at the tormented expression on the girl's face as she wondered what was going on inside Isabel's head. Janet wondered why Isabel had been spared her mother's fate; she wondered if the killer had a more diabolical plan for her.

The girl made her way through the hot, humid jungle; an orange light filtered down from the canopy high above her head. There were eerie sounds around her – multicoloured flying insects buzzed around her. She was sure there was a monster waiting in the emerald green vegetation to pounce on her. Monsters that were intelligent – they attacked swiftly and silently. She had yet to run into the top predator of the alien jungle – she knew they were biding their time; let the insects feed on her first.

Suddenly a tall, slim female figure moved out of the trees across her path; deep set yellow eyes studied her with interest. Her skin was light orange and slightly translucent.

The skull was domed with a thin layer of blonde hair on top. The muzzle was full of long sharp teeth – two long fangs hung over the bottom lip. The girl was ready to run as the tall female predator approached – she hoped it was not too hungry and would leave her alone.

A clawed hand gripped her left arm, a long thin red tongue ran over the two long fangs. She felt the hot foul breath on her face. The yellow eyes stared hard at her, as if it was trying to get inside her head. The head moved down, the long red tongue ran over the girl's face and neck. The alien female was about to feed on the girl – when a blur of movement on one side of them showed the coming of something else that was just as hungry. A taller greyish figure came into view and seized the alien female predator and with flashing talons and sharp teeth, it tore the luckless female predator apart.

The girl now released moved away from the feeding frenzy – away from the sound of ripping flesh and crunching of bones; as the male jungle creature continued to feed on the live meal. The girl had seen the battle of the sexes in this jungle world was savage and deadly.

The girl moved against some vines and they started to encircle her body. The plant life was just as carnivorous, as the creatures in this jungle and the vines were after her blood. The vines wrapped round her body tighter – she tore at the leathery tendrils with her fingers and nails. She did not want to be on the vine's menu. A few moments later the large greyish nightmare came towards the struggling girl and saw her predicament. It tore the vine tendrils from the girl's body – the bright amber eyes stared deeply at her. The girl received terrible alien visions in her mind. The alien killing machine was telepathic.

Helen walked into the bedroom. Janet was sat at the bedside. Helen gave her a mug of tea. She stared down at the sleeping face of her cousin and wondered what horrors Isabel was visualising in her dreams.

"If Isabel is anything like you, Helen, she will pull through," Janet said.

"Thank you for that, Janet – Isabel had good luck when she found you as a friend, Janet," Helen said.

The girl came to a rocky hillside and found a cave. She entered it and went down a rocky passage that was damp and cool. An odour of death and decay assailed her nostrils as her feet squelched in the thick mud that covered the floor of the passage. She came to a pile of bones – that told her something had not escaped the terrors of the jungle. A few steps later she ran into another two corpses. They were female and wore long orange gowns. The girl moved on and the mud got thinner until it left her walking on the bare rock. She came upon a female sat on the cold rock with her back against the rock wall; her feet were tied together, and her hands were tied behind her back. Bright lilac eyes stared up at the girl; she wore a light green gown that covered her slim body.

The girl heard a sound behind her, and she moved to one side. Two amber eyes flashed at her – the male jungle creature reached out for her. The girl moved backward away from the alien nightmare – the ground fell away and she screamed as she fell into the dark pit. Then something grabbed her hand.

Seeing stark terror in Isabel's face Helen grabbed her hand and squeezed it gently. The hazel eyes flashed open and stared at Helen.

"It's all right, Isabel, you are safe now," Helen said.

"You saved me, Helen."

Isabel relapsed into unconsciousness.

Isabel woke from a long nightmare-free sleep. She turned her head and saw Janet sitting at the bedside.

"How are you feeling?"

"Rough," Isabel said.

Janet left the room and went downstairs to let Helen know her cousin was awake.

Isabel told them about her nightmare dream about the alien jungle planet. Janet was interested in the grey creature in her dream – she was sure it was the one she had seen in the woods and that came out of the cottage when she went to visit Isabel.

"You don't think I killed my mother – do you, Helen?"

Helen shook her head. "Of course I don't – the forensic evidence tells us you were held down on the bed; while the killer did his awful work."

DI Peter Hunter came in to question Isabel about the murder of her mother. It was not easy to go through the terror of that night – Hunter told her to go through it at her own pace. As she spoke of her ordeal; Isabel gazed at her cousin, who gave her a smile of encouragement. She described the killer as a tall, dark figure but she could not make much of the features in the dark room.

"After killing my mother, he dragged me to my room – I can't tell you what he did; but it was painful, and it took all night," Isabel said.

CHAPTER 16:

A CHANCE OF A LIFETIME

JUNE 2112

Isabel Eastham and Janet Hodgson were having breakfast together in the kitchen. Isabel was much better, and her mind was in a hurry to get back to work. When they had finished Helen came to call and told Isabel she had some work for her to do. Helen told Isabel she would be going to the Installation – someone would come there and give her some work to do.

"I don't know how to thank you, Helen – you are so good to me."

Helen gave her a hug. "You know how much I care for you."

They left the cottage together and got into Helen's car. Janet got in also as she had a job in the Installation – as did her brother. Helen drove to Cook's farm and then went onto the cliff top Installation. Helen parked the car by the central main building. Helen took her cousin into the building and made for the main offices, where she introduced Isabel to Dr Emily Stuart who told Isabel she would be in the genetics research laboratory – with her cousin Donald; she was happy about that.

"If my reputation has arrived first – I promise you I will give you no trouble."

Emily gave her a broad smile. "Helen has spoken up for you and that's enough for me. I'm sure you will fit in nicely."

"I hope so, I'm glad to have this opportunity to prove myself," Isabel said.

"Someone high up has to hear of your work - they have something important for you to do."

They left the building and Helen got in her car and drove away. Dr Emily Stuart took her to the genetics research building. Janet followed them; they went into the laundry room and Isabel received a white lab coat to put on. Dr Stuart took her to the laboratory. Celeste Barnet was sat at the computer work desk and she stood up as they approached her.

"This is Isabel Eastham – she will be working with her cousin," Emily said.

"I hope you will like working with me," Isabel said.

"If you are anything like Donald, I will," Celeste said.

Dr Emily Stuart told Isabel, Celeste was a good worker and she would assist her in every way. She left to let the two girls get acquainted with each other.

"I'm a bit rougher than my cousin, but I will appreciate all the help you can give me," Isabel said.

"That's OK, we need people like that here," Celeste said.

Isabel liked the younger girl – she told her about the cloning research she was doing. Celeste was impressed.

"Will you be OK with that?"

"Of course – I find your study most interesting," Celeste assured her.

"You are definitely my kind of assistant."

Celeste took her to meet her brother – who she had to give a blood sample to. Nigel shook her hand and told Isabel he was honoured working with Donald's younger cousin. Donald came into the laboratory and gave Isabel a hug. "I am glad Helen got you here, Isabel, you will be a great asset to the team," Donald said.

"We need your DNA for our records," Celeste said.

"I'd like to see the result as soon as you have it."

"It's good to see you up and about – I have been very worried about you," Donald said.

"You don't mind I am not really your cousin?"

Donald kissed her on the cheek. "I know Uncle loved you very much – Helen and I still think of you as our cousin."

Isabel was glad Janet was going to be working with her.

Rosalind Hartsfield walked out of school and down the road. A car drew up to her and stopped. She turned and then opened the door and got in.

"Hello David, I was wondering when you were coming to see me."

Rosalind closed the door and put on the seat belt. David drove off up the road. She had changed her name and she lived in a house in Exeter – bought for her by David – and he got her a place in a local school. When David was not there, Patricia Evans and Sheila Watkins were there to keep an eye on her.

"A lot has been happening, so, I have been busy," David said.

David drove out of the built-up area. Rosalind wondered what he had to tell her. After a short drive David turned off the road and went up a driveway alongside a house.

They got out and Rosalind opened the front door. Rosalind took off her school blazer and hung it up; she followed David into the kitchen. He made some coffee and Rosalind sat at the table. He put a mug of coffee in front of her and he sat on the other side of the table. Rosalind was more content with her life – David and his friends had helped her to get back on her feet. She was working hard on her schoolwork – she was ready to make something of herself. She was not frightened of her shadow anymore.

"I fear no evil," Rosalind said.

"Here – there is no evil after you – you don't have to fear your father any longer," David said.

"There have been other murders?" Rosalind reminded him.

"Someone has an agenda and doesn't care if he has to kill to get it."

"How are you going to flush him out?" Rosalind inquired.

David smiled – her special mind was at work. Rosalind was sure by his smile that she was to provide the answer.

"I'll tell you all that has gone up to date, and you tell me what you think."

Rosalind grinned at him. "As usual I am listening carefully," she said.

They set about preparing and cooking the evening meal – David talked as he worked, and Rosalind listened to all he had to say.

Isabel woke to the sound of someone knocking on her door and she sat up in bed.

"Come in," she called. Janet stepped into the room with a mug of tea. She handed it to Isabel.

"Thank you. You are a life saver."

"I'm glad we are working together," Isabel said.

"So am I, you are a good friend, Janet."

Janet sat on the side of the bed. "We had a message come through. Someone important is coming to see you – so I thought I'd better give you a call."

"Helen told me something like that – I didn't mean to sleep late."

"That's all right, no one expects you to get stuck in straight away," Janet said.

Isabel sipped her tea. "It's nice to have such understanding staff."

"You are Donald and Helen's cousin – that's all we need to give you our support," Janet said.

Isabel finished her tea and got out of bed. She had a shower and got dressed and put on the white lab coat. She walked into the corridor followed by Janet.

When they got to the laboratory, Isabel saw Donald working on the computer. Nigel gave her a sheet of paper.

"That's your DNA results."

Isabel thanked him and took the sheet of paper. They went to see Donald.

"Let's go through the other DNA tests – to see if there is anything strange in them," Isabel said.

Donald and Isabel went to the filing cabinet where the DNA results were kept, which were catalogued by Donald Eastham and Celeste.

Melissa Davis walked into the laboratory and Celeste took her to meet Isabel, the new scientist working with them. Isabel was glad to meet her, as Helen had told her about Melissa.

"I heard about your mother's murder," Melissa told her.

"We had a stony relationship, I reminded her of an affair she had."

"I'm sorry to hear that," Melissa said.

Isabel told Melissa about her dream of the alien jungle and its frightful inhabitants.

"The killer made a link with you and showed you a vision of his planet," Melissa said.

Isabel stared at her. "Do you think the killer is not of this world?"

Melissa smiled and told her there were lots of strange stories about the woods.

"I sense a bond between you and Celeste – what we have experienced – I could certainly use your help here."

Melissa smiled. She had only just met Isabel, but she was sure she was going to like the older girl.

"I'll be only too pleased to help the cousin of Helen and Donald."

Melissa left the laboratory. Janet Hodgson helped Isabel and Nigel to work out the DNA tests and Celeste was sent to help Donald and see why he was sent to them.

CHAPTER 17:

PRODUCT OF TWO WORLDS

Isabel woke and got out of bed and went and had a shower; then she got dressed and put on the white lab coat and left the room. She walked down the corridor towards the laboratory. Dr Emily Stuart came through the entrance doors and approached her.

"Your visitors have just driven through the main gate."

Isabel went into the laboratory and found Donald working at the computer work desk.

"You are a person who likes an early start," Isabel said.

Donald smiled and nodded.

"I've got someone coming to see me," Isabel told Donald.

Isabel left the laboratory.

Isabel stood outside the building and watched a large armoured dark green van move slowly towards her. It parked down the side of the building and a young woman leapt out of the cab – she wore a brown jacket and matching skirt. She approached Isabel.

"You must be Isabel Eastham."

Isabel nodded, and they shook hands.

"Are you the important person I have to meet?"

Tracy Morgan shook her head and asked if there was a back door to the research building. Tracy guided her to the back of the van and opened the back doors. Tracy told Isabel to get in and closed the doors up behind her. She faced a tall, blonde young woman who was sat beside a transparent life support capsule, containing a still, blonde baby girl. Isabel stared at the deep-set sapphire eyes – there was something about her that Isabel found familiar.

"I am Dr Sally Hamilton – I have seen your work and I am intrigued."

"Thank you," Isabel said.

A smile spread over the thin lips. "I have a job for you."

Isabel moved closer to the life support capsule and stared down at the baby girl.

"What's up with her?" Isabel asked.

"I don't know, it's a mystery – she has a twin who is alive and kicking."

"What do you want me to do?"

"The twins have a destiny – if this one does not come out of the coma, I'll have to have her cloned."

The deep-set sapphire eyes stared at her intently; Isabel had an idea of what was expected of her.

"If you think I'm worthy."

Dr Hamilton gave her a thin smile. "Your theories tell me you are, and I could use your help."

"I'd be honoured; it's a chance I'm looking for," Isabel said.

Isabel had yet to find out something about the young woman – but this was the chance of a lifetime and she was going to take it.

"Good," Dr Hamilton said.

The back door opened, and Tracy Morgan told Dr Hamilton all was ready. Isabel helped the tall young woman to carry the life support capsule out of the van and round the back of the research building. The back door was open, and they entered the building. Tracy closed the van doors and followed them in. Janet Hodgson stood by an open door – Tracy had encountered her when she had entered the building by the rear entrance. Tracy asked her way to the medical room.

The life support capsule was placed on a large work top. Isabel told Dr Hamilton that Janet was her assistant and could be trusted. She came under the stare of the sapphire blue eyes.

"I had learnt of the disastrous death of your mother – I'm sorry for your loss."

"Melissa thinks the killer is not of this world – do you think there are aliens in the Universe?"

The tall young woman gave Isabel a strange smile. "Don't you?"

"I think there should be, but I have not seen one yet."

Dr Hamilton placed a hand on Isabel's shoulder. "You have now."

Isabel and Janet exchanged mystified glances.

"My twin girls are a product of two worlds," Dr Hamilton said.

CHAPTER 18:

KNOW YOUR ALIENS

"You are telling us you came here by spacecraft?" Isabel inquired.

Dr Hamilton explained to Isabel she had crash landed on Earth with her mother four years ago and Dr Stanley Hamilton found her at the side of the road and took her to the military installation he worked at. She worked with him and they eventually married, and she gave birth to twins soon after.

A girl about Isabel's age came in wearing a nurse's uniform.

"This is Hilary Rogers, she will be assisting us," Dr Hamilton said.

Janet left the room and went into the laboratory – Brendan Goodman was standing outside the door, and he came up to her.

"What's going on?"

Janet shook her head. "You'll have to ask Isabel."

David had gotten in touch with Brendan and told him someone important was coming to visit them, from the Exmoor Research Facility. He could not tell Brendan what was going on.

As they got ready to start the cloning process, Isabel asked Dr Hamilton who was going to provide the eggs. The ova would be removed from a host patient; they would be treated with ultra-violet radiation to destroy the nuclei. Then the ova would be ready to accept new genetic material.

Dr Hamilton smiled at Isabel. "I was hoping you'd provide them."

Isabel nodded her head. "I had a feeling you were going to say that – it fits my own agenda, so that will be fine."

Isabel went to the operating table and lay down on it. Hilary Rogers came over to her and administered the anaesthetic and waited for Isabel to slip into unconsciousness; then she joined Dr Hamilton.

Isabel woke from an anaesthetic sleep – which featured alien visions of a land of ice and snow and a spacecraft landing on a primitive planet.

"Bad dreams?" a female voice inquired.

Isabel turned her head and saw the nurse Hilary standing by the bed. She sat up in bed.

"You could say that," Isabel said.

Hilary gave her a glass filled with a light green liquid.

"Drink this – Dr Hamilton says it will make you feel better; you can trust her, Isabel."

Isabel sipped it and made a face. Hilary gave her a smile, then she turned and walked to the door and left the room. Sometime later Dr Hamilton came in and asked her how she was feeling.

"All right – I had some bad dreams."

The tall young woman sat on the side of the bed. Isabel told her about the jungle planet and the ferocious wildlife that inhabited it. Looking at the pale thin face; Isabel was sure Dr Hamilton knew what she was talking about.

"You look as if you have heard of the place," Isabel said.

Dr Hamilton nodded. "In the solar system where I come from there are three planets, the one closest to the sun is the jungle planet in your dream. The second planet belongs to the Monox – who are the enslavers of my people, who came from the third planet. My mother and I managed to escape them in one of their spacecrafts. There was a great plague that started to kill off the Monox females; they tried to use the predatory females on the jungle planet, to domesticate them so they could take the place of their dying female stock."

"They must have found it hard to mate with those homicidal females, though the males seem worse," Isabel said.

"They were hard to catch, and they came against the males – they attacked rapidly and none of the Monox who came across them could say what the males looked like. Only you have seen one to tell the tale."

"They are telepathic – that's why I get the dreams," Isabel said.

"We of the Moran think the Monox were evolved from the jungle females – they are quite intelligent if you forget their feeding habits. The Monox enslaved us because they weren't getting much success with the jungle females. There is a race we call the time-shifters – they arrived in the solar system before us – they landed on the other side of the jungle planet from the ferocious life forms. Every millennium a mystery race we call the Marauders, they rush through the Galaxy raiding and plundering planets – some say the time-shifter aliens were searching for the Marauder home planet."

"Their knowledge would be handy to Marauders – they could attack planets in any time they choose," Isabel said.

"Perhaps they are trying to avoid that happening, that's why they are lost in time."

Isabel told her about the murder of her mother and the attack on her mind and body.

"He seems to be my father – I hope it does not mean I will turn into a homicidal maniac."

Dr Hamilton smiled and ran a soothing hand over Isabel's cheek.

"I don't think you have to worry about that – from what Helen has told me about you, you are more interested in your career, than killing people."

"He seems to have evolved in his time on this planet. There's one of those males here – I wonder how he got here," Isabel said.

"That is a mystery – we'll have to ask him when we catch him," Dr Hamilton said.

"Good luck in that – my friend Janet saw him, and it was just a grey blur," Isabel said.

Dr Hamilton left the room. A few moments later the nurse Hilary came in and asked Isabel if she was hungry.

Dr Hamilton entered the laboratory and saw Tracy talking to Donald, at the computer work desk – she went over to them. He found the tall young woman impressive and awe inspiring. The deep-set sapphire eyes stared sternly at him.

"We won't interrupt your work while we are here," Dr Hamilton told him.

Donald nodded and thanked her for helping his cousin. Tracy Morgan left the building and saw Melissa and asked the girl how she was getting on with Brendan Goodman.

"Fine, we are working together on my mother's research."

Tracy smiled. "Brendan is like everything round here; all is not what it seems."

"You are not wrong there," Melissa theorised.

At midnight Melissa took her nightly trip to the woods, but she came across no killers, alien or otherwise – they seemed to have lost interest in finding her alone in the woods at night. She returned to the Installation and the guard let her in and she went back to her quarters.

CHAPTER 19:

SHIRLEY GALLAGHER

Helen Eastham drove along the winding road as the rain came steadily down. The headlights shone through the darkness. Helen kept her concentration on the road ahead; it was just as well her senses were alert, as the car approached an opening in the hedgerow on the left side of the road, a young girl shot out and stopped as if transfixed by the bright headlights. Helen swerved round her and parked on the other side of the road. She got out and approached the girl. Helen could see an expression of stark dread on the girl's pretty face.

"Something is after me – something nasty."

"Nothing is going to hurt you now," Helen told her.

The young girl wore a white blouse and grey skirt.

"What is your name?"

"Shirley Gallagher," the girl replied.

Helen guided the girl to her car and sat her in the back seat; then she crossed over to the other side of the road. She went down the track the girl had emerged from. Helen took the gun out of the inside pocket of her jacket and got ready to face the danger, whatever it was. There were trees on both sides of the track. At the end of it she came to a small cottage.

The front door was wide open; she went in and stood in the hallway, listening for any sound. Helen held the gun firmly in her right hand, as she stepped into the first room. A woman lay on the floor covered in blood. Her keen senses suddenly felt danger – she turned and saw a blur of movement coming down the stairs. She fired two shots at the tall grey figure that shot out the open front door. Helen took out her mobile phone and contacted the police; then she made her way back to the car. The girl was glad to see her.

"Did you see it?" "I saw something – it moved at a fast rate," Helen replied.

The police vehicles arrived, and Helen got out of the car, as DI Hunter approached her; DS Sanderson and PC Rachel Robertson came up behind him. Helen told him what had happened, and Rachel got in the car beside the young girl.

"Are you hurt, darling?"

The girl gazed at the PC. "The monster did not catch me."

"You must be a very fast young lady."

The girl nodded. Rachel thought the young girl had a strong mind.

Helen showed the police officers the way to the cottage. She told him about the mystery figure she had fired two shots at.

"I think it was Isabel's mystery attacker."

"What was he like?" DI Hunter said.

"The figure moved too fast for me to get a good sight of it," Helen said.

"Let's hope the young girl can give a better description," DS Sanderson said.

"Her name is Shirley Gallagher," Helen told them.

Helen stayed outside the cottage, while the police officers entered the building. John Walsh the forensic pathologist came along, and she told him DI Hunter was in the cottage. He went into the lounge and looked down at the body of the woman. DI Hunter was looking round the room. DS Sanderson found the second body in the main bedroom. The death was as violent as the woman's; the girl had been lucky to escape being the third victim.

DI Hunter came out of the cottage and told Helen about what had been found in the cottage; he asked Helen if she had any ideas regarding the sort of killer they were looking for.

"Some – but you won't like them."

Helen went back to her car and PC Robertson got out and crossed the road; Helen asked the young girl if she had any relatives nearby. Shirley shook her head and told Helen she wanted to stay with her. Helen decided to take her to the Installation until they could find some relatives of the girl's parents. Helen drove through the main gates and headed for the main central building; she parked the car and got out.

Helen went to the genetics research building to see how her cousin Isabel was getting on. Shirley followed her into the building, and they went into the laundry room, where they found Melissa, she gave Helen and Shirley a while lab coat to put on, Helen asked her if she could look after Shirley, while she went to see her cousin. They walked out of the room and Melissa told Helen where she could find Isabel, then she took the girl into the laboratory and introduced her to Nigel and Celeste.

"I'd like to take a sample of your blood, if you don't mind," Nigel said.

Shirley pulled up the sleeves of the white coat and blouse. She watched Nigel slid the needle into her arm.

She watched her blood enter the syringe.

"You are a brave girl," Melissa said.

"After tonight, a needle in the arm is nothing compared to what I have just witnessed," Shirley said.

"What was that?" Celeste inquired.

"A monster came and killed my parents – it was not fast enough to catch me."

"What was it like?" Melissa asked.

"It was seven feet in height, it moved like lightning, and was all claws and long teeth."

Melissa and Celeste exchanged glances.

"I don't suppose anyone will believe me – I know the police didn't," Shirley said.

"Two people here will believe you; I am one of them, we had a similar experience," Melissa said.

The bright grey eyes stared at her. "If you saw it – they can't help but believe me," Shirley said.

"We'll back you up, Shirley," Melissa promised.

Helen entered the medical room and Isabel was glad to see her and told her what Dr Sally Hamilton wanted her to do. The first part of the cloning process had been done. Helen told her about Shirley and the murder of the young girl's parents.

"Where is she now?"

"Melissa is looking after her," Helen said.

Isabel went to her room and saw Tracy standing outside.

"Shirley Gallagher's night of horror must have brought back bad memories," Tracy said.

"It was not dissimilar to what happened to me – luckily she was able to run away."

"The sooner it is caught the better." "It seems to want to stay in the same area," Isabel said.

"It kept you alive – perhaps it wants you for some reason."

Isabel had already thought about that.

"It's good you have me to protect you," Tracy said.

Isabel smiled at her. "I'll keep that in mind."

Tracy followed Isabel into the quarters, and they had coffee together.

Melissa gave Shirley a mug of coffee. They were in the rest room – David Walker came into the room. She told him about the attack on Isabel Eastham and the murder of her mother.

She told him about Shirley Gallagher and what she had been through.

Melissa took him to the laundry room and went to the cupboard and took out two white lab coats and gave one to David and they put them on. They left the room and went into the laboratory. David went to see Donald Eastham, who was sat at the computer work desk – Janet Hodgson was sitting next to him. Melissa went to see her friends, who were sitting at their desks on the other side of the room. They were interested to see David again – though they did not know much about him.

"Your friend has come to see you again," Nigel said.

"David has more interesting things to see, than me," Melissa assured him.

"What is more important than you, Mel?" Nigel argued.

Melissa smiled. "There are the people that Isabel is working for – to name a few."

"You never did tell us what work David did," Celeste said.

"There's not much to tell – Brendan was working with my mother on something secret and they sent their findings to David, via Tracy and her armoured van. It was on a need to know and I was not to know – that's why Brendan is so secretive, it's in his nature and job," Melissa explained.

"Why don't you go over there and learn what the two men are talking about," Celeste said.

Melissa gave her a wink and strolled over to the computer work desk. They two men stopped talking.

"Talking about me again?" Melissa asked.

"I was just telling Donald all the activities you have been getting up to," David said.

"I hope you weren't expecting him to believe it," Melissa said.

"Concerning you, Mel – I'd believe anything," assured David.

"Janet, Isabel and Shirley have seen it – Helen could not explain clearly what she saw; it exists, but we can't explain it," Melissa said.

PART TWO:

SECRETS

CHAPTER 20:

DEATH COMES CLOSE TO HOME

JULY 2113

Tracy Morgan drove her large armoured van through the open main gates and headed for the genetics research building that had been enlarged to a long single-storey building. Dr Stanley Hamilton sat beside her – he had come to visit his wife, who was still working on her cloning project. Tracy parked the van and they got out and walked through the entrance door. They went to the laundry room and put on a white lab coat. Then they went down the corridor and entered the medical room. Dr Sally Hamilton was glad to see her husband and took him to the three life support capsules. He gazed at three similar baby girls.

"Why three?" he asked.

"I have to make sure at least one survives – our original offspring may yet wake up."

"Samantha keeps asking when she is going to wake and be friends with her," Stanley said.

Sally smiled and introduced him to Isabel, who was talking to Tracy.

"It's a privilege to work for Sally – she has given me a chance to further my career," Isabel said.

"I hope you get all the success you crave for. Sally has informed me of the good work you have been doing for her," Stanley said.

Isabel smiled and told him she enjoyed the work very much. She turned and saw Tracy leaving the room – she chased after her.

"Are you leaving us?"

Tracy nodded. "I shall be back tomorrow."

"Could I come with you? I am at a loose end now," Isabel said.

"Of course – it's nice to have a companion," Tracy said.

They left the building and got in the cab of the van. Isabel put on her seat belt. After settling herself Tracy put on her seat belt and drove to the main gate. Tracy drove out of the compound.

"Do you carry a firearm?" Isabel inquired.

Tracy kept a tight grip on the steering wheel with her right hand and reached out with her left hand and opened a compartment and pulled out an automatic – she dropped it on Isabel's lap. Tracy placed a hand on her right thigh and Isabel tapped it with the gun.

"It's best to keep your hands to yourself when the girl is armed."

"You can't shoot me while I'm driving," Tracy said, logically.

Tracy put her left hand back on the steering wheel and concentrated on her driving. She got onto the North coast road and sometime later she came to a large patch of trees. She turned down a track and entered a clearing in the wood.

There were two long bungalows. She drove up to the nearest. They got out of the van and Tracy looked up and opened the front door; Isabel followed her into the bungalow and closed the door behind her. The bungalow was a large L-shape – they stood in a long spacious hallway.

"Nice pad," Isabel said.

"I'm glad you like it," Tracy said.

Tracy opened the first door on the right – Isabel saw the room was a small washroom.

Tracy washed her hands and face. She dried them and then moved out, so Isabel could do the same. From there they went to the third door on the left and they entered a large spacious kitchen.

"Will you have lunch with me?" Tracy asked.

Isabel accepted her kind offer and sat on a high stool; Tracy went to the coffee machine and made two cups and gave one of them to Isabel; who sipped while she watched the young woman move round the kitchen as she fixed lunch. Tracy had become a good friend to her; even though she was still a bit of a mystery woman.

"You must have a great wage for being a van driver."

"I like to live in luxury," Tracy confessed.

"You can say that again. Do you plan your covert operations here?"

Tracy laughed and stared at her.

"You are going to make yourself a fortune one day, Isabel. I can see it coming."

"I hope you are right."

"I am. Dr Sally Hamilton is very impressed with your work," Tracy said.

A car drove up to the second L-shaped bungalow and parked by the front door. A tall slim girl got out of the car; she shook her long brown hair and gazed towards the other bungalow. She went to the front door and opened it. A tall dark figure emerged out of the bushes, at the left side of the bungalow – with a rush of speed it hit her in the back and knocked her down on the hallway floor. The end was swift and final.

After they finished lunch Tracy wanted to go out for a walk and asked Isabel if she would accompany her. She nodded, and they left the cottage – it was a warm night. Tracy looked over at the other cottage; she saw the door was open. She walked towards the bungalow and Isabel followed her. They walked round the car and Tracy gazed at the open door, she saw a pair of feet protruding from the bottom of the door.

Tracy went to the door and Isabel stayed by the car. When Tracy stood by the door, Isabel could see her horrified expression and she took the mobile phone from her dress pocket and contacted the police. Tracy had her automatic in her hand as she told Isabel to stay by the car. Tracy went around the building looking in the windows – she saw no one in any of the rooms. She returned to Isabel. Two police vehicles drove up to them and two familiar men got out of the first one.

"Hello Miss Eastham," DI Hunter said.

"It seems we have found another murder for you," Isabel said.

The forensic pathologist came out of the second car; followed by PC Rachel Robinson.

"Hello Isabel, have you found another body for me?" John Walsh inquired.

"Not by choice," Isabel said.

Isabel told DI Hunter that Tracy was the owner of the other bungalow. DS Sanderson followed the forensic pathologist to the body of the girl lying on the hallway floor.

DI Hunter faced Tracy. "How well do you know your neighbour?"

"I have socialised with Sue on occasions – she is a lawyer."

"Have you seen any strangers about lately?"

Tracy shook her head. "All is quiet and still – that's why I live here."

"Not now it isn't," DS Sanderson said, as he came up to them.

"Did she die in the same manner as my mother?" Isabel asked.

Sanderson nodded. "It looks like it."

Tracy walked away and took her mobile phone out of her skirt pocket.

"We haven't seen anything; it did not come after Tracy. It seems discriminate in the target it chooses," Isabel said.

"So, if we find what links the murders, we should get a profile on the killer," DI Hunter said.

"That's what I will be doing – as I carry on with my cousin's research. I'll need a sample of the dead girl's blood for her DNA," Isabel said.

Isabel saw Tracy standing by her bungalow; she walked over to her. DI Hunter turned to PC Robertson.

"What do you think of Tracy Morgan?"

"She is a smart young woman, highly intelligent – cagey about giving information about her," Rachel said.

"And sexy with it," DS Sanderson said.

"That is obvious," Rachel said.

DI Hunter decided to find out more about Tracy Morgan. He watched her talking to Isabel – a car appeared and drew up to them.

David walked out of the car and went to Tracy. A teenage girl got out of the passenger door. DI Hunter stared hard at her as she stood by the car. After a short conversation David walked towards the police detectives. He showed his ID card.

"I'd like to have a look around the bungalow – if one of your officers can accompany me."

DI Hunter told Martin Sanderson to go with David. "I'd like to have a word with Miss Taylor," DI Hunter said.

"Of course, she has changed her name – she wanted to get away after her mother was killed and Rosalind had an idea that she would be next."

"We will be gentle with her," Rachel said.

David nodded and made for his associate's bungalow; DS Sanderson fell in step with him. Rosalind watched the police inspector and the PC walking towards her. She wondered if he would be mad at her for disappearing and not telling the police she was alive and well.

"I'm sorry I did not tell you I was safe and well – but I was in danger and I had to get away."

"Can you tell me what happened?" Hunter asked.

Rosalind explained to him how her father was acting strangely before he ran amok and killed her mother and then ran after her in a boiling rage.

"He had some idea I was not his – even though Mother had a DNA test on me to prove it."

"Why would he think that?" PC Robertson inquired.

"My hair and eyes are different to my parents – and my skin complexion," Rosalind said.

Entering the bungalow, David went into the room that was used as an office. He went to the desk computer and looked through the files that Sue had on it. DS Sanderson walked round the room and found it a well-ordered office room. He walked back to David and he told him there was nothing on the computer to suggest any reason for her murder.

"Did she have any friends?"

"There was Jemima Hitchens – she works for me and was a close friend at college. She visited Sue here on many occasions – Tracy has met the girl," David replied.

David left the bungalow and returned to the car – where Rosalind was waiting for him.

"Shall we go for a walk?"

Rosalind nodded and followed him to the dead girl's bungalow, and they walked down the side and then went to the tree line.

"It went this way," she said.

DS Sanderson left the bungalow and joined them. They walked a short distance then Rosalind stopped and faced David.

"It shot off at a fast pace from here – it could be anywhere."

"I don't suppose you got sight of him?" Sanderson inquired.

"It was only a grey blur," Rosalind said.

"It doesn't look as if we are chasing anything human," Sanderson said.

The grey eyes with the lilac flecks stared hard at him.

"No, it doesn't," she agreed.

David and Rosalind got in the car and he drove away. Tracy returned to her bungalow and Isabel followed her into the kitchen and sat on a high stool. Tracy made coffee and put a drop of brandy in the mugs and handed one to Isabel.

"Did you know the dead girl well?"

"We had lunches together and we talked about the legal work she did, especially if she needed my help for anything," Tracy replied.

"I'm sorry for your loss," Isabel said.

DI Peter Hunter ran through the police database for information on Tracy Morgan – she had not committed any crimes, as far as the police records were concerned. He went to the civil database and found out she had done well at university and she was a highly intelligent young woman. Her employment was stated as a delivery driver for Military and civil scientific establishments. Tracy owned a firearm which she was licensed for. As he started to dig deeper into her life, alarm bells rang, and he got 'access denied'.

Hunter then received a call from the Home Secretary to inquire why he was investigating Tracy Morgan. Hunter told him about the violent murder of Tracy's neighbour, and that she was not accused of anything; they had to rule her out as a suspect.

"Does David Walker know about the murder?"

"Yes – he drove up as we got there," Hunter replied.

"He'll get someone to interview Tracy – there are certain things she can't tell you about herself."

"I have a friend of the dead girl to find and question – so I'll start with her," DI Hunter said.

After breakfast the doorbell rang. Tracy left the kitchen and Isabel stood by the window and stared at a large dark limousine, with dark tinted windows – the owner must have secrets to hide, Isabel thought.

"Curious and curious," Isabel muttered.

Tracy opened the door and stared at the tall lean man that stood outside – he wore dark glasses and had a thin smile on his lips.

"Have you been a naughty girl, Tracy?"

He pushed past her and stood in the hall.

"Have you been murdering your neighbours?"

Tracy shook her head. "No, I haven't – I hope you haven't been telling the police I have."

The man shook his head and smiled. "The police are interested in you – so we had to put them off."

"That's very good of you."

"I just wanted to make sure you weren't involved in your neighbour's death," the man said.

"Now that you know I had nothing to do with it, was there anything else?"

He gave her a cold smile. He knew there was no love lost between the pair of them – he could live with that – they had different agendas, even though they always seemed to clash, even though she tried to avoid him like the plague. He turned and walked out of the bungalow. Tracy shut the door and turned – Isabel was standing just behind her.

"Who was that?"

"Just an irritating person – who wants to know if I killed my neighbour," Tracy replied.

The man got in the car and a young blonde woman with blue eyes stared the engine.

"Tracy has a new friend."

"Will that be a problem when I try and get hold of Isabel?"

"No – I can soon get Tracy out of the way," he replied, confidently.

The young woman gave him a smile – everything was going to plan. The man had contacted her a year ago. She was glad he had heard of her and wanted to make a partnership with her. They both had their agendas and she was sure he would be ideal for her purposes. He told her of his campaign to gain power for himself and it was going to include her as well. She learnt he was devious and ruthless like her and did not mind getting rid of people who were in the way. She was a scientist and he needed her knowledge.

Tracy watched the car drive away, then she left the bungalow with Isabel. They got in the van to drive through the trees and onto the coast road. Sometime later Isabel looked in the wing mirror and noticed the black limousine behind them.

"We're being followed," she said.

Tracy sighed and kept driving until they got to Horner Wood; then she turned off the road; the black limousine kept on the road and shot off; Tracy felt relieved as she drove down the track. It led her to the Exmoor research facility. Tracy showed her pass to the security guard; Isabel showed him her ID and the pass for the Installation. He let them through, and she made for the main administrative building. They got out of the van.

"Is this another secret scientific establishment?" Isabel asked.

"This is where Dr Sally Hamilton works," Tracy said.

Tracy went around to the back of the van and opened the doors; she picked up a large cardboard box and handed it to

Isabel and told her it was heavy. Isabel took the weight and then waited for Tracy to pick one up and she followed the young woman across the compound.

They entered the Lab 1 building and walked into a large room with several desks with computers on; a girl sat at one and a man stood beside her; when he saw Tracy, he walked over to her. She introduced Dr Albert Harris to Isabel.

"You are the clone girl – we have learnt about you."

They put the boxes on two empty work desks. Then Isabel walked over to the girl working on the computer. She gazed at the data on the screen.

"That looks complicated," Isabel said.

The girl turned to her and smiled – the grey eyes with lilac flecks flashed at her.

"They are the doctor's new teaching machines and I am the first guinea pig."

Dr Harris came over to Isabel and asked her if she wanted to have a go.

"Why not," she said.

Tracy went into the office and found David Walker sitting at the desk. She told him about the visitor that came to her home.

"They told me someone was going to see you. Did he give a name?"

Tracy shook her head. "He followed us here – then went on his merry way."

"We'll have to find out more about your mystery man," David said.

Tracy smiled and wished him luck.

CHAPTER 21:

A MURDEROUS PARTNERSHIP

SEPTEMBER 2113

When Dr Sally Hamilton went back to the Exmoor research facility, Isabel went with her. They worked in an underground laboratory – the ginger-haired twin was down there with them. She was sixteen months old and she was very inquisitive – as Isabel was new the girl followed her about the laboratory, asking questions about her work with her mother. She was eager to learn all Isabel could teach her.

Dr Albert Harris was glad to see her again and got her to try the teaching machines again – as she had done so well the first time Isabel tried them in July. He was impressed with how fast she solved the problems and thought she was highly intelligent. Dr Hamilton asked her how she was getting on and Isabel told her that she did not find them a problem.

One day she decided to take a trip to the Installation and Tracy drove her there. Melissa Davis was glad to see her and wanted to know all about the new place she had been to.

"Why don't you go back with Tracy – I have a few things to do here; I'm sure Dr Hamilton can give you some work to do," Isabel said.

Isabel told her about Dr Harris and his teaching machines and told Melissa she should have a go with them while she was there. Tracy was very happy to take Melissa with her, as it would be company for her.

When they were on the coast road a large black car with tinted windows turned up behind them. Tracy drove off the road and parked on the grass and the car shot past them. Tracy waited until it disappeared, then she drove back on the road.

"Do you know them?"

"Not yet – now he is just an irritation," Tracy said.

"I might be able to help you out there," Melissa said.

Melissa told her that the car came to the Installation on occasions and when she was off the compound visiting some friends the car had been lurking about in several areas.

"If I see them again I can ask them what they are up to."

Tracy smiled – the girl had guts even though she had no idea what she may be getting into.

"You'll have to tell David about that idea before you do anything rash."

Tracy drove her van into the Exmoor research facility and parked by the administrative building. David was standing outside waiting for them. Tracy told him the black car had followed her again and Melissa wanted to do something about them. Tracy told him of Melissa's plan.

"Can't you ever find a less dangerous occupation?"

"I have the killer of my mother to find – perhaps I'm stronger than you think," Melissa said.

"This girl has a very strong will and a determined nature," Tracy said.

David stared hard at her. "If you do anything, make sure Brendan is watching your back."

Melissa nodded and then David took her to the teaching machine room and introduced her to Dr Albert Harris. When he showed her to the machines, she saw a girl sitting at one who looked familiar.

"Ross?"

Rosalind turned her head and smiled. She stood up and Melissa hugged her.

"I thought we had lost you," Melissa said.

Rosalind was glad to see Melissa – she was missing her old friends.

"I'm sorry I did not let you know I was safe – I just had to get away."

"I understand. It's just good to see you safe and well," Melissa said.

Melissa sat at one of the machines and Dr Harris stood over her and gave her instructions of what to do. He praised her work and Melissa told him she wanted to do as good as her friend Isabel. Dr Harris assured her there would be no problem with that. After three days of hard work, Melissa went out for a walk. She got to the road and the large black car with tinted windows drew up to her. The back door opened.

"Hello Melissa, would you like a lift?" a man's voice asked.

"You know me?" she asked.

Melissa looked in the back of the car – it was dim, and she could not see the man clearly. He told her it was safe to get in and she did so. She closed the car door – she saw a blonde woman in the driving seat.

"Yes, we have met before. Where are you off to, Mel?"

She tried to see his face, but he kept his head turned slightly away.

"I was just going for a walk," Melissa said.

"I have admired your hard work – you are a credit to your mother."

"Do you know who killed her?"

"Not yet – but I am still looking into it. I have an important job to do and I hope I can call on you to help me if I need it."

"Are you some sort of secret agent?" she inquired.

"Something like that – there's a lot of important research being done at the Installation."

"If you find something I can do for you, I'll do it," she said.

"Good, I'm glad to hear it. I know you are determined to find out who killed your mother and Brian Scott – I can help you with that."

"Thank you. I'm staying at the Exmoor Research Facility for a couple of days," she said.

"I'll turn up and give you a lift back," he said.

Melissa got out of the car and shut the door and walked down the road. She heard the car drive off.

"Do you think she will help our cause?" the blonde woman asked.

"Mel will be able to give you an idea of what Isabel Eastham is doing for Dr Sally Hamilton," he said.

When she got back to the Exmoor Research Facility, Melissa told David and Tracy about her meeting with the man in the black car with tinted windows. David was disappointed she could not describe the man and she had not seen the face of the woman driver either. He did not like the idea of these people picking her up and driving away.

"He's supposed to be a government agent – Tracy says he is an irritant; we don't know anything about his female driver. I can find out what his agenda is. He did not sound if he was going to murder me," Melissa said.

"Mel is a very stubborn young lady," Tracy said.

"I knew you would be fighting in her corner," David said.

Tracy gazed at Melissa. "Mel reminds me of myself when I was her age."

"He showed no signs of wanting to harm me – he knows about my work, so he must have worked at the Installation at some time."

Melissa spent her time working with Dr Harris's teaching machines and giving Dr Sally Hamilton some help in the underground laboratory. The little girl with ginger hair and bright green eyes seemed to be glad to see her – she bombarded Melissa with questions about her knowledge.

OCTOBER 2113

When she left the Exmoor research facility and got onto the road, the large black car with tinted windows turned up and the back door opened.

"Are you going our way, Mel?" a man's voice inquired.

The back door opened and she got in, closing the door behind her. The blonde woman was once again the driver; they went steadily along the road. The man had the hooded garment on and dark glasses that obscured his face from her. He asked her what she had been up to and she told him about Dr Albert Harris and the work she was doing with his teaching machines. The man told her that he knew him. She told him of her work with a tall strange blonde woman in an underground laboratory.

"Dr Sally Hamilton?" the woman asked in a Scandinavian accent.

"Yes – my friend is helping her with some cloning experiments."

"Isabel Eastman?" the man asked.

"That's right – have you heard of her?" Melissa asked.

"I was there when she joined the scientists at the Installation. You can help us get these people we are after – it's not one killer we are after," the man said.

"Do you think there is a conspiracy? Melissa asked.

Melissa asked him to drop her off at the village. When she got to the Installation she told Brendan about the man and woman in the dark car and her hope that she would eventually learn who he was and what he was up to.

"You're taking a chance – getting into a car with two unknown people," Brendan said.

"Well you will be watching my back – that's what David wants you to do," Melissa said.

Melissa told Celeste and Nigel – they hoped she was not going to do anything bad; they did want her to get locked up. Melissa left the building and went to the Microbiology building. Dr Emily Stuart was there; they were both glad to have her back again.

"I suppose Dr Harris got you working on his teaching machines," Emily said.

"Yes – he said I was good – but not as good as Isabel," Melissa said.

"I expect the machine malfunctioned," Dr Stuart said.

Melissa hugged her. "Thank you for that."

At the end of the day Melissa asked Brendan if he would have lunch with her. He accepted her kind offer, and Melissa took him to her quarters where he helped her fix lunch. After they had eaten, they sat on the couch and drank coffee.

"You are going to trust me now?" he asked.

"Of course. David wants us to work together," Melissa said.

The next morning when Brendan and Melissa entered the Microbiology research laboratory and saw Isabel there, she told them she was going to see DI Hunter. Melissa offered to go with her and Brendan told them he would drive them to the police headquarters. Isabel went to see Dr Emily Stuart to tell her what she was going to do.

"Let me know what you find out."

"I will," Isabel assured her.

They left the building and walked to the car.

"Had you met Tracy's neighbour – the girl that was killed?"

Brendan nodded.

"I received her DNA results and I want to get the DNA of other victims like her, from the police pathology lab," Isabel said.

"Do you think there is a link?"

They got in the car and Isabel sat in the back seat; Melissa sat beside Brendan. He started the car and drove out of the compound.

"It is part of my cousin's research – Donald had the idea. I'll know more when we have seen the pathologist, John Walsh."

DI Hunter was glad to see the two girls safe and well. Isabel told him what she wanted and hoped he could help her.

"Of course – any help we give you might help us overall."

"I sincerely hope so," Isabel said.

They entered the forensic lab and DI Hunter escorted them to John Walsh's office. He was glad to see Isabel looking well.

Isabel told him what she wanted, and he showed her the DNA of the victims killed in the same way as Tracy's neighbour.

"It's hard to find a motive for these killings," DI Hunter said.

"What about DNA being the motive?" Isabel said.

"That's beyond me," Hunter said.

"That's an interesting hypothesis," John Walsh said.

Isabel gave Walsh her DNA results. "The killer is part of me – I don't want to turn into a homicidal maniac."

"You won't," Melissa assured her, and she turned to DI Hunter.

"There is also the death of Bruce Taylor," Melissa said.

"Have there been others like him?" Dr Walsh asked.

"Melissa's father tracked down two before he disappeared, and Marina was working on the problem," Brendan said.

DI Hunter studied Brendan. "Do you think that's the reason she was killed?"

"It's possible – that's why we want to keep Melissa in sight at all times," Brendan said, as he gazed at the girl.

Isabel turned to Brendan – he obviously knew more than she did.

"Do you think these two cases are linked?" Isabel asked.

"Your cousin seemed to think so," Brendan said.

"Is Rosalind in danger?" DI Hunter inquired.

"Rosalind is a very remarkable girl. She is being monitored – she is helping with the research into her father's death," Brendan said.

At the end of the day Brendan ran the two girls back to the Installation. The large black car turned up and followed them for a while then drove down a track off the road.

Two days later Isabel returned to the Exmoor research facility to work with Dr Sally Hamilton. She told David about the visit to the police forensic lab and how they were followed when they left.

"The car is leased to several drivers – they are being checked out," David said.

"Check which one of them goes around with a blonde woman driver," Isabel said.

Isabel went down to the underground laboratory to continue her work with Dr Sally Hamilton.

The next day Isabel went for a walk. When she got to the road she looked out for the dark car with tinted windows – but it did not turn up. However, instead a small green car did and drew up to her. The driver was a woman – she was alone.

"You are Isabel Eastham?" she asked.

Isabel was wary as she nodded her head.

"I wonder if I can speak with you – I have a cottage not far away."

"I don't know you – what do you want to talk about?"

"I want to talk about your work. I am a doctor and you interest me. I assure you, Isabel, I have no reason to harm you."

Isabel thought for a moment then walked round the car and got in the passenger seat and put on the seat belt. The woman drove for a mile then she turned off the road and parked along the side of a small cottage.

They went in through the back door and stood in the kitchen. The woman made some tea and they went into the lounge and relaxed on the couch; Isabel was more at ease as they sat and sipped their tea.

"What type of work are you doing with Dr Hamilton? Your friend Melissa told us you were working with her."

Isabel studied the woman – her face was pretty and the blue dress she wore hugged her curvy body.

"Dr Hamilton wanted me to help her clone one of her baby girls; it was in a coma – in case she did not come out of it," Isabel explained.

The woman studied Isabel's face. "Was the cloning successful?"

"At the moment it seems that way," Isabel said.

The woman smiled at Isabel. "You are being very cooperative – I like that."

"You said you weren't going to harm me – somehow I believe you," Isabel said.

The woman smiled and stood up and carried the empty cups to the kitchen; Isabel followed her.

"I'll drive you back to the facility," the woman said.

They left the cottage and got in the car. The woman drove to the facility and dropped Isabel off. She told nobody at the facility about her meeting with the blonde woman.

Melissa made her way along the roadside until she got to the track that led to the two houses; between them on the gravel path was the large black car with tinted windows. She went to the one on her left and rang the doorbell and waited. After a few minutes the door opened, and she stepped into the hallway. A tall blonde woman stood beside her.

"It's nice to see you again, Mel – go into the lounge."

Melissa went into the lounge. It was dark except for a lamp close to an armchair on the other side of the room; she sat down. The man came in and closed the door and went and stood behind the chair. He was taking every precaution to make sure she could not recognise him.

He asked Melissa how she got on at the Exmoor research facility. Melissa told him she did fine, and Dr Harris said she was a good student.

"I want to know if there is anything strange happening there," he said.

Melissa felt she was being interrogated.

"Won't they let you in?" Melissa inquired.

"I don't need to – I have you to get information for me – I shall pay you."

Staying behind the chair he dropped an envelope in her lap, which she picked up and then walked to the door.

"I'll contact you later for more information you can get me."

Melissa walked out the door and out of the house. When she got to the top of the track a car pulled up and she got in the passenger seat. She showed Brendan the brown envelope.

"It's a profitable business this information gathering."

"Let's hope he gives you some information for a change," Brendan said.

"You and David give me the questions and when he trusts me, I will ask them," Melissa said.

Brendan kissed her on the cheek. "You can guarantee that?"

"I think so – only time will tell," she said.

A few days later Isabel was walking along the road and the green car drew up to her again. She got in and the blonde woman drove up to the cottage and they had tea in the lounge.

"I can help with your cloning research."

"That's all I want to do is carry on with my research," Isabel said.

The woman smiled.

"You can do that. I will take you to a laboratory that will give you everything you would require."

"The offer sounds a good one – we will have to trust each other," Isabel said.

Isabel studied the woman's face – it had strong features. She was sure the woman had plenty of strength in her tall, slender athletic body. Isabel was sure the woman was honest in her proposal to help in her research.

"I don't mind who I work for – as long as I get what I want," Isabel said.

"I'll drink to that," the woman said.

CHAPTER 22:

DR BRIAN STONEHOUSE

JANUARY 2114

Erika Strausberg drove into a housing estate and went to the other end and parked close to a large grey stone two-storey house. She gently nudged the sleeping girl on the passenger seat beside her.

"Wake up, sleepy head."

Isabel woke and looked about her. "Are we here?"

Erika nodded, and they got out of the car and walked to the front door of the grey stone building.

"Dr Stonehouse will provide you with all you need – he has a large laboratory," Erika said.

Erika rang the doorbell and a few minutes later a girl in her early twenties wearing a nurse's uniform opened the door. She smiled when she saw Erika.

"It's nice to see you again, Miss Strausberg."

Erika and Isabel stepped into a large spacious hallway.

"Thank you, Miranda – is Dr Stonehouse free to see us?"

Miranda Miles was twenty, she had a slim figure. She guided them to the other end of the hall and opened a door on the left. They entered a large luxuriously furnished office. Dr Brian Stonehouse sat behind a large desk. He was in his early thirties and well built, dressed in a brown suit. He stood up and gave Erika a hug and told her it was good to see her again. He looked at the beautiful well-built girl beside her wearing a lime green dress.

"This is the girl I told you about."9

Erika introduced him to Isabel Eastham and he shook her hand.

"I hope we have an excellent working relationship."

"I hope so, too," Isabel said.

"Miranda will show you the well-equipped laboratory that will be at your disposal. Miranda will guide you in the ways you can help her, and she will assist you in your projects, when she can," Dr Stonehouse said.

Isabel smiled. "Thank you – that would be much appreciated."

"Miranda will show you to your room."

Isabel followed Miranda out of the office and down the hall to the front door.

"Nice pad," Isabel said.

Miranda opened the door and they went out to the car. Isabel opened the boot of the car and took out her large suitcase. They entered the building and Miranda guided her up a large winding staircase. They turned left and entered the first door on the right. Isabel placed the suitcase on the bed.

"It's nice to meet you, Miranda – I hope we can be friends."

Miranda gave her a hug. "I don't see why not – the work is hard, but interesting; we shall make a great team."

Miranda left the room and Isabel removed her dress, then her socks and trainers. She went to the adjoining bathroom and had a shower. Then she went back to the bedroom and unpacked her suitcase and put her clothes into the large wardrobe.

She got dressed and left the bedroom. She found Dr Stonehouse outside waiting for her. He guided her to the other side of the landing, and they went up some stairs and went into a doorway and entered a large, spacious laboratory. Isabel marvelled at the medical equipment in the room.

Miranda was standing by the door. Dr Stonehouse asked Isabel what she thought.

"It's amazing. I shall enjoy working here."

"Excellent. Miranda will show you around," he said.

Miranda took her to the end of the landing and went up another flight of steps. They went into a small room and handed her a nurse uniform to put on. She took off her dress and Miranda took it and hung it up in an empty locker. Isabel put on the uniform. They went through another doorway and entered a laboratory and Miranda showed her around; she told Isabel how the various instruments and machinery worked and how they were used. Miranda told Isabel the jobs she would have to do to help her. Isabel assured Miranda she would give her all the assistance she needed. They went down to the ground floor and went to the kitchen and had a meal together.

Isabel soon got into the swing of things – she worked in the laboratory running the blood samples Miranda gave her. Miranda worked with Dr Stonehouse with the mental patients who lived in the housing estate. Isabel worked with their DNA – she was back doing her cousin's research. Was the key to the patients' mental problems in their DNA? In the first week she did not see the doctor as she worked full-time in the laboratory on the jobs Miranda gave her and she sent the results down to the doctor. Miranda would tell Isabel he was well pleased with the work she was doing.1

After a few months Erika came back to see how Isabel was getting on with her cloning experiments. Dr Stonehouse joined them and was intrigued with Isabel and her work – he told her there was some other work she could do for him. Erika stayed with them as she had some work for Isabel to do.

Frederick Fairclough had breakfast with his father – his mother had died mysteriously. When they had finished Patrick went off to work and Frederick went into the lounge – a few minutes later the doorbell rang, and he went out to answer it. On the doorstep stood Judith Johnson.

They went into the lounge and sat on the couch – at thirteen Judith was a year younger than her neighbour; they went to school together. She lived with her mother – her father had run off with another woman when she had been eleven. They lived at the far end of the housing estate – away from the large grey stone house. They had had their first visit there the day before.

"That was a strange experience we had at the large grey house," Frederick said.

Judith smiled and had been glad her friend had been with her when strange examinations were done on their person. They had blood tests and brain scans – the doctor did not tell them what he was looking for; he just told them it was precautionary.

JUNE 2115

Melissa Harris had married Dr Albert Harris the year before –now she had given birth to a baby girl whom they named Juliet. She was happy because she had received a text from Isabel congratulating Melissa on her marriage and the birth of Juliet. Isabel did not tell her where she was but told her she was safe and well. She contacted David Walker – Melissa was sure he would like to know Isabel had made contact.

David Walker drove up to the large grey stone house. Dr Moira Banks sat beside him, Rosalind sat on the back seat. He parked the car and they got out and David rang the doorbell; Miranda Miles opened the door. David told her he wanted to see Dr Stonehouse. Miranda took them to the office. Dr Stonehouse stood up and shook David's hand, then he turned to Dr Banks whom he had met before.

"It's good to see you again, Moira."

Dr Banks introduced him to David and Rosalind.

"There's something we hope you can help us with," she said.

Dr Banks gave him a file and he sat at his desk and looked through it. Rosalind went to the window and looked out – it had started raining.

"We have had a few cases – we wanted to know if you have come across anything like this," Dr Banks said.

When Dr Stonehouse had read the file he looked up at Dr Banks. He told her there had been a couple of cases similar with his patients. Dr Stonehouse stood up and guided them out of the office and up the stairs and to the end of the landing, then they went up the steps to the laboratory. A man and Isabel were there in white coats; and Dr Stonehouse gave his visitors a tour of the laboratory and showed them what he had found out about the two cases he had come across. Rosalind watched closely – she was interested in the tall, stout doctor, she wondered what the others were thinking about him. She turned to the male laboratory assistant – there was something about him that unnerved her. Dr Stonehouse showed them the electron microscope. They stared at the screen. David turned to Moira and she nodded. The culture was like the one that had infected Bruce Taylor.

When they were back outside Rosalind walked down the side of the house. David called out to her to find out where the girl was going. At the rear of the house was a large lawn and gardens – beyond that was the wood. Rosalind stood at the tree line and David stood beside her.

"One wood looks the same as another," David said.

The grey eyes flashed at him. "I'll have to educate you on that. Terrible things happen in that house," Rosalind said.

David smiled at her. "Moira and I have already detected that."

Rosalind laughed and kissed him on the cheek. "There you are, my influences are working on you at last. I will soon have you thinking like me."

"I shall look forward to that," David said.

They walked back towards the car. She asked him if he had spoken to Isabel. David told her the girl had said her cloning research was going well.

"We'll have to keep an eye on that," Rosalind said.

They walked to the car and found Dr Moira Banks there waiting for them.

CHAPTER 23:

ESP

JULY 2121

Jocelyn Wotton stood and stared out of her window at the woods beyond the back garden. She thought of the strange things that might lurk amongst the trees and in the undergrowth. She was fourteen and had a very vivid imagination. Her mother told her someone was coming to see her and test her for special talents. Julie Wotton was worried about her daughter, even though Jocelyn had assured her mother that there was nothing wrong with her.

Jocelyn left the bedroom and exited the house by the back door. She wore a dark green dress, long lime green socks and brown trainers. She walked along the path by the side of the lawn and made for the tree line. She moved into the wood and made for her favourite spot in the wood and sat down and laid her back against a tree. The sun flittered through the tree tops.

An hour later Julie Wotton left the house and walked down the path to the tree line. As she got there Jocelyn came out of the woods. She hugged her mother.

"Were you worried about me?"

They walked towards the house. "Mothers are always worrying about their teenage daughters," Julie said.

They entered the house and Jocelyn sat at the kitchen table. Julie made some tea and placed a cup in front of her daughter.

"Thank you, Mother," Jocelyn said.

The doorbell rang, and Julie went to answer the door. Frederick Fairclough gave her a warm smile as she let him in the house. He worked at the Exeter Experimental Laboratories – they were testing young people for special talents in mind and body.

They went into the kitchen and Julie introduced Fairclough to her daughter. She smiled at Fairclough as he sat opposite her.

"How are you, Jocelyn?" Fairclough asked.

"I'm doing fine, thank you," she said.

Julie put a cup of tea in front of Frederick; he sipped it as he studied Jocelyn – as she munched a sandwich. He waited for her to finish it, then he asked her some questions – Jocelyn was happy to talk about herself. Fairclough learned she had good school reports and there was no trouble there – she liked roaming the woods and being close to nature. He asked Jocelyn if she had any strange feelings about the world around her. She looked at her mother and Julie gave her a smile.

"When Jocelyn plays in the wood, she is in her own private world," Julie said.

"Even the young have secrets – Jocelyn is a very bright and intelligent girl," Fairclough said.

"Mother worries a lot about me; I wouldn't do anything to hurt her," Jocelyn said.

Fairclough got up and Julie saw him the door. He told Julie she had nothing to worry about – Jocelyn was an exceptional young girl.

"You've put my mind at ease – I was getting worried about her."

Fairclough left the house and went to the other end of the housing estate and made for the grey stone house. Miranda Miles opened the door and took him to see Dr Stonehouse.

"Hello Mr Fairclough. How did it go with Jocelyn?"

"You were right about her – she is a remarkable young lady," Fairclough said.

Dr Stonehouse smiled. "I knew you'd like her."

Fairclough told him they would start testing Jocelyn next day. Dr Stonehouse asked Fairclough to keep him informed about Jocelyn's progress. Fairclough assured him that he would.

The next day Fairclough went to see Jocelyn Wotton. Julie opened the door and let him in. She took him into the kitchen where Jocelyn was sat at the table; she smiled at Fairclough.

"How is my star pupil?" he asked.

"I'm fine," Jocelyn said.

Fairclough told Julie he was going to take Jocelyn to the EELto be tested. He told Julie about the work he was doing with young people, to see if they had any hidden talents. He hoped Julie would come too, so she could keep an eye on her daughter.

Melissa Harris drove through the main gates of the Exeter Experimental Laboratories and stopped the car in one of the parking places on one side of the boundary fence. Sitting beside her was Juliet; who was now six. They got out of the car and a young woman approached them, followed by a blonde girl the same age as Juliet. Caroline Clarke was glad to see her friend again – her daughter Janice grabbed Juliet by the hand and the two girls ran towards the living quarter buildings.

"It's about time you visited us again, Mel – Janice has been missing her friend," Caroline said.

"The ESP tests they are doing here interests some of my friends and they want me to look into it," Melissa said.

"I'll take you to the testing room," Caroline said.

They walked to the main building, which was single storey and covered a large area. They entered the air lock; the shutter came down behind them. The inner shutter went up and they stepped into a small room where they approached the reception desk ahead of them. The security guard gave Melissa a smile when she handed him her ID card.

"Long time, no see, Mel – are you coming to work here?"

Melissa nodded. "I was told there was interesting work for me to do here."

"Good – it's great to see you again," the guard said.

Frederick Fairclough entered the testing room, followed by Julie Wotton and her daughter. There was a long table in the centre of the room – a male and a female sat at either end of the table. They had a head set on that was connected to a machine in the centre of the table. Dr Samuel Hendricks stood by the young man; Tabitha Dawson stood close to the blue-eyed slender female. There were couches along one side of the room and Julie took her daughter to them and they sat down. Fairclough went to Dr Hendricks.

Fairclough took Dr Hendricks over to meet Jocelyn Wotton. The girl gazed up at them as Dr Hendricks told Jocelyn what he wanted her to do.

"I shall enjoy working with you," Jocelyn said.

"I hope so," Fairclough said.

Julie and her daughter stood up and followed the two men to the conference table. Tabitha fitted a monitor to the machine and the young girl kept close to her. Suddenly pictures appeared on it – showing images of what the machine had taken out of the minds of the subjects they had tested.Caroline Clarke and Melissa Harris walked into the room and approached the table. Melissa was glad to see Hector again. She noticed the small girl that stood close to Tabitha Dawson and Susan Bishop. Fairclough introduced her to Jocelyn.

"This is Melissa – she is a sensitive."

"Is that good?" Jocelyn inquired.

"Yes, Joss – Melissa is just like you," Fairclough told her.

Jocelyn smiled at Melissa. "Do you explore the woods, like I do?"

"Yes, I was always exploring the woods when I was younger."

"Are you a country girl, Mel?" Julie asked.

"I was born in the city, but we moved into the country soon after," Melissa said.

Fairclough smiled at her. "Do you think there's a difference between people brought up in the cities and the country?"

The bright brown eyes flashed at him. "Mother seemed to think so; city people are not close to nature, like I am – that's why people think I'm strange."

"I don't think you are strange," Jocelyn and her mother said together.

Melissa went to the small girl who was standing close to Tabitha.

"How are you getting on here, Wendy?" Melissa inquired.

"Very nice – have you seen Daddy?"

Melissa gave her a hug. "Yes – he will be coming to see you soon, Wendy."

Jocelyn and her mother sat at the table. Fairclough and Dr Gilligan put the girl through several tests to see if they could produce some ESP from the girl – Jocelyn was very cooperative.

Dr Emily Stuart and Susan Bishop left the room; they turned right and walked down a corridor and at the end they entered another room and got into a lift that would take them down to the underground level. When the lift stopped, they got out and walked down a long corridor and at the end they entered the storeroom. They turned left and went through a doorway that led them to the laboratories.

Dr Moira Banks approached them and took them through an air lock – they removed their outside clothes and put on a white lab coat. They went through another air lock that took them to the maximum containment laboratory. Dr Banks took them to a bench where an electron microscope was situated,

Emily looked at the screen. She could see the culture had been genetically engineered.

On the other side of the laboratory the air lock door slid open and Susan Bishop turned and saw Rosalind walk into the room – she held a small girl by the hand – followed by David Walker.

Rosalind introduced Dr Stuart and Susan to her five-year-old daughter, Natasha – the girl had the same features as her mother, right down to the grey eyes with lilac flecks.

Susan asked Dr Banks if Rosalind and her daughter were healthy. She told Susan they were fine, and they were being monitored all the time. 0

Melissa Harris walked down the corridor and one of the living quarter's doors opened and the guard she met at the reception desk came out.

"It's about time you came to see us, Mel," he said.

She gave him a smile. "I'm a busy lady."

He could see she looked dead on her feet.

"If you haven't been assigned a room yet, you can rest here – I have a lot of rounds to complete, so I won't be here to disturb you," he said.

Melissa entered the quarters and the guard left her to rest. She undressed and got into bed. She gazed up at the ceiling. Melissa thought about the test she had just experienced with the girl Jocelyn. Dr Sally Hamilton had contacted Dr Gilligan and got him to organise the tests with Frederick Fairclough to find young people who had ESP potential. Something dark was coming and Dr Hamilton wanted people with talents for telepathy and telekinesis and other paranormal abilities.

Melissa wondered if she had any magical powers – if she had, they had not shown up yet. Perhaps if she faced extreme danger, they would come to her – Melissa had shuddered at the idea. Melissa had been tested with Jocelyn and she got several impressions of the girl in her mind – when she had the headset on, she was sure Jocelyn was sending some of the thoughts to her. Tiredness put her into a restless sleep that brought about a strange dream.

Two men were carrying a body into the woods – their faces were shadowed by the dim light. At a certain place they put the body down and one of the men dug into the dark earth with a spade. Then they lay the body in the shallow grave; then they covered the body up with dark earth and dead vegetation.

Melissa woke up and sat up – her body was covered in a cold sweat. She had a shower and got dressed and left the quarters. She went to the testing room where she found David Walker and she told him about her dream. She described the clothes the body was dressed in – then she told him about the tests she had had with Jocelyn Wotton.

Frederick Fairclough had taken Julie Wotton and her daughter home. David Walker decided to go and see them – he told Melissa to stay where she was. David drove back to the housing estate and Rosalind sat beside him. Natasha sat on the back seat.

"By your expression, something bad is about to happen," she said.

"We have a body to find and I think it's Melissa's father."

"That is bad," Rosalind observed.

"Yes – it is," David agreed.

Julie Wotton opened the door – Frederick Fairclough stood behind her. David asked her if he could speak to Jocelyn. She looked at Fairclough and he told her it was all right. Julie let him in. Rosalind went around the back of the house and walked down the garden path to the wood beyond the garden. She walked through the trees and she came to where Jocelyn sat against a tree; Rosalind sat beside her.

"Have you come to be my friend?" Jocelyn said.

"I hope so," Rosalind said.

Rosalind told her about the dream Melissa had had after the testing.

"Have you any secrets, Jocelyn?"

Jocelyn thought for a moment. "There are a lot of secrets in this wood."

Rosalind took a photograph out of her blazer pocket – David had given it to her to show the girl. Jocelyn studied it.

"Yes, I remember him – he was around asking questions; he went around the houses," Jocelyn said.

"Do you remember where you saw those two men in the woods?" Rosalind asked.

Jocelyn nodded. "Were they doing something bad?"

Rosalind nodded. "As bad as you can get," she said.

Jocelyn moved round the tree she had been sat against and Rosalind followed her. They went a short distance then Jocelyn looked about her.

"Somewhere here," she said.

Rosalind looked about then did a circuit around the nearby trees –then she stopped and stared at Jocelyn.

"This is the place," Rosalind said.

Jocelyn came to her and stared at the pale face – she saw the lilac flecks in the grey eyes for the first time.

"You are more remarkable than me," Jocelyn said.

Rosalind smiled at her, knowing they had made a connection between them. Rosalind told her to go back to the place they met, as her mother would be there. Rosalind rang Patricia on her mobile phone and learnt she had contacted the police and they had just entered the wood. David Walker came into view and Rosalind showed him the location of the shallow grave.

"You never cease to amaze me," David said.

Rosalind gave him a beaming smile. "You've known me long enough to have learnt all my secrets."

Rosalind walked away and went through the wood towards the other end, where she would meet up with Patricia Evans and the police, who were walking up the path towards the tree line.

Rosalind led them through the wood; DI Hunter and his sergeant and the forensic pathologist came up behind. Rosalind led them through the woods to where David Walker was waiting for them. He had uncovered the body with a spade, and he stood waiting for John Walsh to study the body.

"I suppose I can take you off the list of suspects," DI Hunter said.

David smiled. "A young girl saw the two men burying him – she's waiting to talk to you."

David told Hunter where he could find Jocelyn and he sent DS Sanderson to interview her.

"I take it you know who the victim is?" DI Hunter said.

"I have an idea, but I want John to verify it," David said.

John Walsh handed the body's ID that he had found in the deceased's jacket pocket, to DI Hunter. He told David who the victim was and that confirmed David's worst fear.

"How did you find out he was buried in the woods?" Hunter asked.

David told him about the ESP experiments; Melissa had been working for the girl Jocelyn – they had made a connection with each other. Jocelyn had given Melissa a memory of something she had seen in the woods.

"Don't ask me how they do it," David said.

"I showed Jocelyn a photograph of Melissa's father and she told me he had been round here asking questions," Rosalind said.

"He obviously found out something that got him killed. We'll know more when we find out how he was killed," David said.

DS Sanderson returned after his interview with Jocelyn – she had given him a good description of the two men she had seen burying the body.

Melissa walked away from the living quarter buildings after visiting her daughter and crossed the compound. A car drew up to her and she stopped walking. Brendan Goodman got out and she took him into the main building and took him to the testing room where Wendy was waiting for him. When he went into the room the small girl exploded from a chair and leapt into his arms.

"I missed you, Daddy," Wendy said.

"I missed you too, sweetheart," he said.

Tabitha Dawson came up to him and Brendan gave her a hug and thanked her for looking after Wendy.

Twenty minutes later Brendan and Melissa got in the front of the car and Wendy sat in the back with Celeste Barnet.

Brendan drove to the housing estate and drove onto the driveway of a house and turned off the motor. They entered the house – Brendan took Wendy to the kitchen; Celeste took hold of Melissa's hand and guided her into the lounge. David Walker and Rosalind were sitting on the couch. Melissa knew something was up.

Melissa walked into the kitchen and Brendan gave her a hug.

"I'm so sorry, Mel."5

"I have closure and two lots of revenge to dish out."

Melissa made herself some coffee and Brendan took Wendy to the lounge. Rosalind got off the couch and took hold of Wendy's hand and guided her to the couch and they sat down.

Brendan went back to the kitchen and gave Melissa a hug.

"I shall be with you all the way."

"Let's go for a walk," she said.

They walked out the back door and walked along the path that led them to the tree line, then they walked parallel with the trees. They reached the last house on the row and Melissa stood and stared at the large grey stone house.

"We'll have to pay the doctor a visit," Melissa said.

Melissa turned and started to walk back the way they had come; at the third house down, Melissa noticed a girl watching them. She started to walk up the path towards them. She was tall and well built; she wore a black top and black skirt – her midriff was bare, and she had a small gold cross fixed to her navel. Her hair was thick and bushy. Her dark grey eyes studied Melissa with interest.

"You are new here."

"I'm Melissa – what is the occupant of the grey house like?"

The girl's face went as dark as her hair and eyes. "A shady character – is Dr Stonehouse."

The girl told them her name was Phoebe Cross and told them of strange things that happened at the house at night. Weird sounds and lights appeared in the woods – Phoebe told them they were haunted. Melissa had heard that before.

"There are woods where we live that are inhabited by supernatural beings," Melissa said.

Phoebe was amazed. "Have you seen these supernatural beings?"

Melissa shook her head. "No – I can't say I have."

"I haven't seen anything like that," Phoebe admitted. "Dr Stonehouse's male assistant is creepy, with amber eyes."

Melissa and Brendan exchanged glances. "Sounds like the subject we are searching for," he said.

"When you get sent to the grey stone house – you don't come out the same person. My father wants me sent there," Phoebe said.

"You don't get on with your parents?" Melissa inquired.

"My father hates me, and my mother ignores me."

Phoebe had thought of running away – but she had a younger sister to protect.

"That's rough," Melissa said.

Phoebe smiled – but there was no amusement in it. "It's going to be rougher."

Melissa silently agreed with her. She turned to Brendan and told him this Dr Stonehouse was worth an investigation. Melissa decided to put herself in the firing line and see if he needed another nurse to help him. Phoebe thought she was taking a chance and Brendan agreed with the girl.

Phoebe moved down the path to her home. Brendan and Melissa moved along the tree line back to the house where they were staying. When Phoebe entered the kitchen two men were waiting for her. Her father and the doctor's creepy assistant.

"Who was that you were speaking to?" Elmer Cross inquired.

"Just strangers asking if it is nice to live here," she said.

Elmer glared at her. "Did they say who they were?"

"They did not tell me their names," Phoebe lied.

The tall thin man moved in front of her – the amber eyes stared down at her; Phoebe moved away from the creepy assistant. Elmer left the kitchen. The amber eyes continued to stare at Phoebe – she was rooted to the spot, as the hypnotic stare got stronger.

"I know you are lying – won't you tell me who they were," the icy voice said.

Phoebe told him that she only knew the girl as Melissa – the man did not mention his name. The expression on the thin face told Phoebe that he knew Melissa.

Melissa told David Walker what she had in mind – he was not too happy about it, but as least Brendan would be looking out for her. Celeste Barnet and Patricia Evans would be keeping an eye on her too.

"If you sense any danger, Mel, I want you to get out of there," David said.

Melissa nodded.

One morning Melissa made her way to the large grey house; Miranda Miles opened the door. Melissa asked the nurse to take her to Dr Stonehouse. Melissa entered the house and they walked down a large hallway.

"Are you unwell?" Miranda asked.

"No, I want to see him about some business," Melissa said.

Miranda knocked on the office door, then they went in; Dr Stonehouse was sitting at his desk and Melissa introduced herself. He studied her as Melissa told him she was a qualified scientist and she had worked with many medical teams. Melissa told him the research laboratories she had worked for. Dr Stonehouse was impressed.

Dr Stonehouse told her there was a job here if she wanted it – she could help Miranda out in the laboratory. They left the office and went up the spiral staircase and then up the steps to the laboratory. After she got a tour of the well-equipped laboratory, Miranda took her to a room where she could change and put on a nurse's uniform. Miranda told Melissa about their patients and their problems. Melissa could sympathise with what they were going through.

Nothing strange happened on her first day and she had to leave the house in the evening; she went to her house and told Brendan about her day.

"At least you weren't changed while you were in there," he said.

Melissa smiled. "I expect Phoebe was talking about the patients not the workers."

"Did you see the creepy assistant she talked about?"

Melissa shook her head. "There were a few strangers working in the house – I did not find them creepy."

They had lunch with Celeste and Patricia. When it was dark Brendan and Melissa went out to the woods. Melissa wanted to know what sort of haunting happened in the woods. Brendan held a flashlight as they made their way through the trees.

"I hope we don't run into any supernatural beings," Brendan said.

"You've got me to protect you – we are not going to a garden party," Melissa said.

Brendan was only too aware of that – he did not want Melissa to get in over her head – they had already lost her parents and he was guarding against Melissa ending up the same way. They exited the wood close to the rear of the grey stone house. There was activity at the very top floor of the house – probably where the laboratory was situated.

Coloured lights flashed in the windows and strange noises could be heard.

"They must be having a party," Brendan said.

"It is bad of them not to invite us," Melissa said.

The back door opened – they dived into the cover of the trees. Melissa detected something moving to her left. Brendan was behind her – the torch that he had held in his right hand was replaced by an automatic pistol. Melissa moved quickly to one side and something bumped into her – then she heard a shot and a howl of pain. Something crashed through the trees and undergrowth heading away from them. Brendan came up to her.

"Are you all right, Mel?"

"Yes – did you see it?"

Brendan shook his head. "It was a blur – it moves fast – but I hit it."

Melissa told him about the grey blur that Janet Hodgson had seen in the woods when she was fourteen.

"I think it was Dr Stonehouse's creepy assistant," Melissa said.

"Just what are we looking for?" Brendan inquired.

Melissa did not say anything and he followed her along the tree line until they got to the house they were staying at. Celeste and Patricia were there taking care of Wendy. Melissa told them what they had seen and heard while they were out.

When Melissa entered the grey stone house, the next day Miranda Miles put her to work. Throughout the day she met some of the patients that came to the house; she could sense the mental problems they were having and they were receptive to her. Dr Stonehouse was impressed with Melissa and he found her a great help to his practice.

Dr Stonehouse was polite to her and Melissa could see nothing underhand or dangerous about his work with his patients. When it was time for her to leave, she took off the nurse uniform and put on her own clothes and then hid in a small room off the laboratory.

When it was midnight she crawled out of her hiding place and left the room. There were strange sounds coming from outside the house. Melissa looked out of the window. Melissa smiled – somehow, she was not surprised as she watched a spacecraft land at the back of the house, close to the edge of the wood.

Their investigation had just got wider than they had anticipated. She was not coming against supernatural beings – but beings from another planet – from another solar system.

David and Brendan aren't going to believe this.

Now Melissa knew what the coming crisis entailed, and she was in the middle of it. Melissa turned away from the window and negotiated her way across the laboratory, until she came to the door – it opened, and the lights came on.

"Melissa. We wondered where you had got to," Dr Stonehouse said.

Behind him was a tall slender female with burning ruby eyes; Melissa stared at her. Dr Stonehouse turned to his companion.

"Melissa is here to learn more about the universe she inhabits."

He turned back to Melissa. "My visitors will be very interested in you, Mel."

Another tall female came into view and was more of a nightmare – it reminded Melissa of Isabel's dream of an alien jungle planet. The creature fitted Isabel's description of the female predator perfectly. She remembered the description of the male predator – it gave her an idea of what Dr Stonehouse's creepy assistant was.

The yellowy eyes regarded Melissa as if she was going to be the next dinner. Melissa stared at the female with the ruby eyes with amazed curiosity; if the female expected fear, Melissa did not oblige her. It was up to her to gain all the information about these alien females that she could.

"I am Zindra – you show strong will and courage."

The voice was a slow vibrating drawl, full of menace.

"Ultimate power is not everything," Melissa said.

A smile flitted over the thin lips. "You are definitely a subject for experimentation."

"After that I get fed to your nightmare friend," Melissa said.

A hiss came from the female creature and the yellowy eyes glared at her.

"You've hurt Zelphas's feelings," Zindra said.

"If the male of her species catches Zelphas, it will be more than her feelings that will get hurt," Melissa said.

The two alien females stared at each other; then Zelphas gazed at Dr Stonehouse.

"You haven't told them about the polymorph?" Melissa inquired of him.

Zindra stared at Melissa.

"I'd like to know how it got here," Zindra said.

"It got here somehow, and it is killing certain people," Melissa said.

Melissa turned to Dr Stonehouse. "What do you know about your strange assistant people have been telling me about?"

He did not answer her.

"I am hunting it and when I catch it – I shall kill it," Melissa said, with a strong edge to her voice, giving the aliens no doubt of her meaning.

"Your hunting days are over – you will be taken to our spacecraft and you will be studied there," Zindra said.

Melissa realised she was never going to see her husband again or her friends; her daughter Juliet would have to survive without her.

Dr Stonehouse gripped her arm and they walked across the laboratory and went through a doorway that led them to an operating room. A girl lay on an operating table – Melissa recognised one of the doctor's mental patients.

Melissa had not found anything dangerous about Dr Stonehouse's practice; until now. She hoped Brendan would not end up like her – for she knew he would be coming to look for her. Melissa was taken to the fire escape door and taken down the steps to the ground; Zindra took hold of Melissa and took her to the spacecraft.

In the morning Brendan went to the grey stone house to see what had happened to Melissa. He saw a car parked close to the front door. Two men came out of the house – he recognised them both. He wondered what they wanted with Dr Stonehouse. He watched the car drive away. He called on Dr Stonehouse who told Brendan that Melissa had left at the usual time – he had not seen her since. He asked Miranda but she did not know what had happened to Melissa.

Brendan went back and told Celeste and Patricia: Melissa was now missing. Brendan took Celeste back to the Installation, then returned to the EEL and took Wendy with him. David Walker was there, and Brendan asked him what he knew of the two men he had seen at the grey stone house.

"Matthew Hastings works for a computer firm in the experimental division; his companion was a security guard who worked here for a time – perhaps you should go and see Hastings; I'll give you his address."

Tracy Morgan answered the doorbell and smiled as she stared at her visitor.

"Nice to see you again – I'm glad you're back at last."

Isabel smiled and walked into the house; she saw Tracy gazing at her bulge.

"You've brought someone with you," Tracy said.

"Yes – it's my destiny and I want you to be a part of it," Isabel said.

Tracy guided her into the kitchen and Isabel found her cousin Helen waiting for her – she gave Isabel a hug and they sat at the table and Isabel told them what she had been up to. Shirley Gallagher made some coffee.